The Emerald Lei

By

Susanne Bellamy

The Heirloom Search

Book 2

(Book 1: The Emerald Necklace by Annie Seaton)

Second edition: The Emerald Lei March, 2019

Originally published as Winning the Heiress' Heart

Copyright © January 2015, Susanne Bellamy.

ISBN 978-0-6484569-9-5

Dedication

To my parents who, like Eva, also accepted the challenge to uproot themselves from England and travel to foreign climes.

Acknowledgements

With many thanks to my CP, Erin, and to Annie and Robin H

for keeping me on the straight and narrow.

SUSANNE BELLAMY

Chapter One

Hawaii 1960

Lucien Martineau pushed open the back door of the plantation house. 'There is Nuthin' Like a Dame' blasted from the kitchen radio along with his cook's slightly off-key singing. Luc hung his fedora on the rack, dropped his suitcase by the door, and sniffed appreciatively. *Roast pork.*

"How long till dinner, Annie?" He leaned around her ample frame and filched a taste of chocolate cake batter from the mixing bowl. *My lucky day when Annie came to work for me.*

She turned, hand on hip, and raised the wooden spoon like a pointer at his chest. "Where you been, Luc? Jack Lyons rang hours ago. Been ringing twice a day since you left. Couldn't get hold of you at that hotel you stayed in."

He paused, hand hovering over the rim of the bowl. Muscles tensed, his heartbeat sped up, hammering like a drum roll in his chest.

The plantation estate sale! Had Benson agreed?

As nonchalantly as he could manage, he leaned back against the counter and folded his arms. "What did he want?"

"Said there's a tenant in the Benson house, that English heiress the papers wrote about, and she needs a hand. Said you were the one to help her."

"Tenant? He's leased the house then?" Jack had earned the bottle of imported single malt Luc had promised if he'd sealed the deal. He pushed off the counter, grabbed his hat, and was almost out the door when Annie called after him.

"Yeah, *heiress* tenant. Dinner will be ready in an hour. Come home any later and I feed that pork to your dog."

Luc zipped back and kissed her cheek. "You're looking at the new owner of the Benson plantation, and that pork will be waiting for me to celebrate when I get back."

Laughing aloud, he skirted the table and raced out the back door. He bounded off the veranda and up the track linking the two estates. If Jack had found a tenant for the house, Benson must have accepted his offer for the land. Which would give him twice the property his father had owned, *and* the best plantation on the island. That meant the Tourism Board contract was as good as his. The contract was in the bag.

His foreman, Sam, met him halfway up the track. "Welcome back, boss. Good news?"

"Yep. You can start clearing that track to connect us with next door."

"Benson sold it to you? I'll get the boys right on it."

Giddy with elation, Luc strode up the hill, brushing past long-fringed palms. Late afternoon sun cast a golden light over the field of spiky leaves, and he paused to admire the rows of plants curving down to meet the track. Hawaii joining the Union was momentous, and if his research was accurate, the Island would be seeing a steady rise in the number of tourists visiting. Soon he'd be bringing in visitors from mainland USA and reaping the benefits of Statehood.

A pity his father hadn't seen eye-to-eye with him about this project. It was one of only a handful of disagreements they'd ever had. But that didn't matter now because Benson had finally forgiven Luc's ill-advised proposal to his daughter, Genevieve, and agreed to sell him the place.

He breathed deeply; the sweet scent of pineapples and success surrounded him. For the first time in years, a sense of hope filled Luc's chest. Finally, everything was working out.

Three distinctive notes of birdcall trilled and were answered from deep within the palm-filled ridge separating his plantation from Benson's. A machinery track had to go through the lower slope to link the fields but otherwise, this forest remnant would remain intact.

Adrenaline pumped through his body as he took the short cut through the palm grove. What a celebration he'd plan. Details for a tourist itinerary jostled in his mind. The two new teenage boys he was mentoring could be trained as guides, and he'd put in the order for the people mover tomorrow. Until it arrived from the mainland, they'd make do with smaller groups in Jeeps.

As Luc crossed the ridge and strode downhill, he wondered why Jack had asked him to help the new tenant. Pity his excitement at the news had stopped him from thinking clearly before he left his house. A phone call to Jack might have easily sorted the problem and he could have been toasting his good fortune right now.

Once he found out what the new tenant wanted, however, he'd head home and have that whiskey to celebrate. Soon.

He rounded the last bend in the track, emerging on the western side of Benson's plantation house. Sunlight bathed the roof in golden light, imperceptibly releasing its hold, until only the weather vane glittered in the last rays. Wide verandas cast deep shadows, but a flash of white near the front door caught his attention.

He climbed the side steps, strode around the corner and crashed into a ladder. Unbalanced, the ladder wobbled. Barely noting his stinging shin, a startled gasp was his only warning before a body dropped into his arms. A very feminine body, all curves and satiny skin and long, auburn hair.

Instinctively, his arms tightened. His right hand slipped down bare thigh below a pair of tan shorts and held tightly while his left hand shaped the curve at the side of her breast. Milky-white skin, soft and smooth as satin, warmed beneath his tanned hands. Slowly, his gaze travelled up the length of woman in his arms.

Strands of auburn hair slipped off her face as she raised her head, and her perfume, complex and elegant, tantalized his nostrils. It had been too long since he'd held such a delightful armful. Luc adjusted his grip and the slide of his hand along silky skin fired up

3

desires he'd ignored since the Genevieve debacle. By rights he should have been embarrassed but right now, an apology was the last thing on his mind. Delicate features, a turned up nose and startled green eyes looked into his. A gentleman would immediately release her. A gentleman would apologize for causing her fall. Instead, he held her against his chest and grinned.

A gentleman missed out on all the fun.

"Hi there. I thought I was the one dropping in."

Rosy-pink flared along her high cheekbones but she gave him a quick smile. "My apologies. I don't usually fall into a man's arms at our first meeting."

Cool and cultured, her English accent explained her delicate colouring. But what was an English rose doing in the middle of pineapple fields?

"Then I am honoured to be the exception. Are you okay to stand?"

"I'm fine, thank you."

Reluctantly, he released her and hooked his thumbs into his pockets.

She took a step back before holding out her hand. "I'm Evangeline Abbott. You must be *Monsieur* Martineau?" Her accent on the French title and his name was that of a fluent French speaker.

He shook her proffered hand, holding it longer than politeness dictated. Warm and soft, it fit snugly within his. "Please, call me Luc. A pleasure to meet you, Miss Abbott."

A pleasure indeed. His skin tingled with the memory of her body plastered against his. It had probably cut Jack to the quick having to ask for Luc's assistance. Knowing his friend's love of beautiful women, Luc had no doubt that, given half a chance, Jack would have monopolized her attention. He'd thank Jack later for sending him up to meet the new neighbour. "You've a fitting name for a newcomer to our little paradise."

A small frown knit her brow and she tipped her head to the

side. "Abbott?"

"Eve."

Her smile tightened and her gaze narrowed on him, cool and assessing. Had he overstepped some undefined boundary? The odd image of a door closing between them settled in his mind. "Don't you like compliments, Eve?"

"Not particularly, and I prefer Eva—to my friends. Mr Lyons said he'd ask you to call on us."

Us? She was married? Disappointment stabbed and he clung to the smile he'd worn since Eva Abbott had landed in his arms. Of course some lucky man would have put his ring on her finger long ago. No wonder his compliment had drawn such a cool response. "I gather Mr Abbott wants to speak with me. Is he home?"

"Mr Abbott?" She frowned before a broad smile took its place. The cool mask fell away and her expression lit up as she pronounced his name. "Oh, you mean Sebastian?"

That Sebastian was the love of her life couldn't have been clearer. Love like that had skipped Luc's family. A band tightened around his chest and threatened to suffocate him. He didn't understand that sort of smothering love. He didn't *do* love.

Eva giggled and his attention snapped back to lush pink lips curved in a smile and the hint of a dimple on her left cheek. Her green gaze met his. "He's not quite eighteen yet, but he'd be chuffed you thought him older."

"Chuffed?" He shook his head and wondered what had happened to his grasp of English. "Forgive me, but I don't understand what you want from me. I thought Mr Abbott wanted my assistance?"

She looked away and her right hand toyed with her left, rubbing her ring finger. It was bare, but she twisted her fingers around it as though she was used to playing with a piece of jewellery. "There is no husband, *Monsieur* Martineau. Just me. Look, would you like a drink while we talk? Mr Lyons said you'd be able to help me with Seb. He's the reason I wanted to speak with you."

Luc nodded and his smile firmed. She wasn't married. There was no husband. Just a teenager who needed help. Jack must have talked to her about his work with Acky and Moe. Was this Seb at risk, too?

Intrigued, he followed her straight back and softly swaying hips as she led him down the wide hallway and through the library. Half-unpacked boxes littered the polished wooden floor. Several contained expensive, leather-bound books, the type of volumes passed down from one generation to the next. The sort of treasures one would ship to Hawaii if they were planning to make a permanent home there. The possibilities opened up by his newest and nearest neighbour were looking better by the minute. "Are you planning to stay a while?"

She turned a steady gaze on him. "Indeed, I hope so. We've sold everything in England."

"A major move then. Do you miss it? Your home, I mean."

She looked through the window. Beyond the house, dusk was quickly falling. She touched her fingers to a pane and Luc sensed she was seeing a remembered scene. A soft sigh fluttered away, so soft he wasn't quite sure if he'd imagined it. "I miss the garden at Bellerose most. Gardenias and roses scenting the night air. I doubt they will grow, let alone thrive, in this hotter climate."

"You might be surprised what flourishes here." Including an English rose, if he had his way.

She blinked, as though the sound of his voice had woken her from her reverie and dropped her hand to her side. "Perhaps. Shall we?" Straightening her shoulders, she led the way into the sparsely furnished reception room.

Gut and fists clenching, he stopped in the doorway. *Not this room.*

The last time he'd been in this room, he'd proposed to Genevieve Benson and she had dumped him. Her dismissal ghosted through his mind and his jaw tightened.

"With a divorce in your family and a mother who's the scandal of the island? How could you ever think I'd consider marrying you, darling? We've had a good time, Luc, but you're not marriage material. Although if you make an indecent amount of money, I'm sure some woman will be only too happy to overlook your shortcomings."

Eva's voice intervened in his dark thoughts. "I'm sorry I can't offer you a selection yet but I have a tolerable sherry. Will you have a glass while we talk?" She stood by the sideboard and waited, hand on a crystal decanter.

Luc forced himself to step into the room and walk to the nearest armchair. Desperately, he scrambled to collect his thoughts. *Never again.* Love was for fools. He looked across at Eva Abbott's curves. A breeze drifted through the open window and carried her scent to him. His arms still held the ghost of her body against his. An affair, however, would be very pleasant.

"Thank you, yes. And my friends call me Luc. I hope we'll be friends—Eva?"

"Perhaps." She poured two glasses of golden sherry and carried one to the small table beside him, carefully placing it within easy reach. "Maybe you'd like to hear the favour I have to ask of you before you offer more."

He sipped the sherry. "Spanish?"

"You've a discerning palate, Mr—Luc."

"I'm more a Scotch whisky man but I appreciate quality, wherever it's from. So, this favour—it has to do with Seb?"

"How did you—of course, Mr Lyons told you."

"I haven't spoken to Jack but his message said you needed my help. I assumed he mentioned the program I've been piloting with the island boys."

She sat and folded her hands neatly in her lap. "He did and it sounds like the answer to my prayers. Please, tell me more. You work with them on your plantation, don't you?"

"They're boys at risk, some of whom would likely end up in jail, but I teach them the ins and outs of growing pineapples and the everyday workings of a plantation. Whether or not they choose to stay with me afterwards, they all develop skills that make them employable."

"Mr Lyons said you've had a great deal of success. He was talking about you turning the lives of those boys around. That's very commendable." She gave him a silent toast and sipped her sherry.

He shrugged then grinned inwardly, aware of the irony. Compliments made him uncomfortable, too. "I offer them the opportunity. If they put in the work, they succeed and they learn that working brings its own rewards."

"I haven't heard of another program like it before. It sounds wonderful, and exactly what Seb needs."

"Bit of a hell-raiser, is he?"

"Not exactly but—he needs more discipline than I can give. Frankly, he needs a man's guidance. I've done my best but I'm not his father."

"Seb's your brother?"

She paused before answering quietly. "Nephew. Phillip—my oldest brother—was killed recently." She dropped her gaze to her white-knuckled hands and drew an audible breath before slowly releasing it. "He was a test pilot. When his plane crashed, I became Seb's guardian." She pressed her lips firmly together before quietly clearing her throat.

"My condolences. That's a difficult task, especially when you must also be grieving for your brother. Do you not have other family to help?"

She raised her glass and sipped before carefully replacing it on the side table. Arms folded across her stomach, she stared at a spot on the rug between their feet. "Harry, my other brother, was lost when his ship was torpedoed early in the war, and Seb's mother and my parents died in the London bombings. The war deprived me of most of my family."

Jaw tight, Luc nodded and frowned. Loss and grief were probably the story for many British families. "The war tore many families apart."

"Pearl Harbour must have been as bad. I guess you know what it was like." Finally, she raised her head and made eye contact.

His stomach clenched as vivid memory rolled back the years. He knew. Twelve years old and free as a bird, he and Jack had camped overnight in Keaiwa Heiau National Park. Early the next morning, they'd used his birthday gift of binoculars to identify the silhouetted shapes of the American Fleet anchored in the harbour. Instead, bombs rained from the sky and fire lit the water. He doubted the memory would ever fade. "They were terrible times."

"Seb's the only family I have left. I'm doing what I can but lately he's become...difficult."

"He's a teenage boy. Most go through a rebellious phase. I sure did." He smiled. Perhaps the personal remark would lift her anxiety.

She gave him a distracted half-smile and interlaced her fingers in her lap. "I understand he's grieving for his father—they were very close, you see—but I fear he might follow in Phillip's footsteps."

"Flying, you mean?"

"I couldn't bear to lose him, too. He's got the same...reckless attitude Phillip had. Combined with a young man's sense of his own invincibility, well... That's part of the reason I decided to sell and come to a new country, somewhere very different from England."

"And take his mind off flying?"

"Yes."

Hesitant to give offence, at the same time he understood the challenge Eva had undertaken. A few tips on raising a young man wouldn't go astray. "Sometimes you have to compromise. It's much better than butting your head against a brick wall."

Her green-eyed gaze flashed with fire, putting him in mind of a lioness protecting her cub. "What are you suggesting I do? Let him take flying lessons?"

"I wouldn't presume to tell you what to do. Just don't hold the reins too tightly. Teenage boys need space to grow into young men." And the chance to make their own mistakes and work out who they are. He'd plant the seed of the idea for now and offer to help if she wanted it.

Slowly she nodded. "I remember how it was with Harry. Tell him not to do something and for sure it was the one thing he would do."

Luc's respect for Eva grew. Taking on responsibility for her teenage nephew was a huge commitment, as was moving them both to a foreign country. A simple offer would ease her concern about her nephew. "How can I help? You want me to give Seb the same training I give the boys in the plantation programme?"

Her body stilled and her gaze settled on him. In her eyes he discerned a yearning to give her nephew the best she could. Right now, it seemed the most important thing in the world to help her achieve that peace of mind. And give him a reason to see more of her? He wouldn't mind that either.

In fact, he planned to see a whole lot more of Eva Abbott, nephew or not.

Even across the intervening yards between their chairs, her tension was palpable. "Would you consider taking him on?"

"I don't see why not. Soon, I'll have a great deal more work with tour groups visiting and if Seb trains up well, he could work permanently for me."

"That's very kind of you, but I hope with the training you give, he'll learn enough to take over the running of our plantation before too long."

"Your plantation? You plan to buy property here?"

"I already own a place. I signed the deed for this plantation yesterday."

Chapter Two

The room blurred and Luc's blood rushed through his veins with an insistent pounding so loud it blocked all other sound.

Eva had bought Benson's plantation?

Heiress tenant. Annie's words leached into his brain. *Heiress.* Finally it dawned on him that she wasn't just renting the house but had bought the whole damned lot. Benson had been stringing him along and never intended for him to have the place. How deep must the old man's desire for revenge go if, after all this time, he couldn't bear for a Martineau to purchase even the fields? Maybe Benson had lost the woman he loved to Luc's father, but that had been over thirty years ago.

For the life of him Luc couldn't put two words together to ask Eva if the contract had been finalized, couldn't think for the crashing of his dreams in this room of lost hopes and desires. First Genevieve had dumped him in this room, now Eva had sealed his fate. Without the second plantation there'd be no Tourism Board contract, no tourists, and no money to expand his program for the boys.

"Luc? Are you unwell? Shall I pour you some water?"

Why had she come along when he was so close to signing the contract? His offer had been generous and he'd been sure he could convince Benson to sell to him. In spite of Genevieve. And his mother. He drew a deep breath and met Eva's concerned gaze.

"I'll be in touch tomorrow. I—good night, Eva." Abruptly, he stood, placed his glass on the table and walked out.

Benson's plantation was never going to be his.

***

Eva stood on the veranda and watched the pale ghost of Luc's retreating back until he turned onto the track and she lost sight of him. With a sigh, she sat on the swinging seat and crossed her legs, pushing just enough to set up a gentle rocking motion.

What had she said to upset him? His face had paled when she'd mentioned purchasing this place.

"How odd. Now why should that information concern him?" And why was she talking to herself?

She balanced her elbow on the back of the swing seat and cradled her cheek in her palm. Really, the whole meeting hadn't gone at all as planned. For a start, Luc Martineau was darkly handsome and much younger than she'd expected.

And she'd fallen into his arms and made that stupid comment.

Cringing at the memory, she instead called to mind those moments in his arms. Strong arms, saving her from a bad fall and holding her longer than necessary. She saw again his chiselled features, felt the rasp of stubble on his square jaw as clearly as if he still held her against his muscled chest. His dark gaze had warmed as his strong hands wrapped around her bare legs and came tantalisingly close to her breast. Dear God, she shouldn't have enjoyed the feel of a stranger's hands on her bare skin.

Heat suffused her cheeks. Even now, her skin tingled at the thought of his hard body pressed against hers and her stomach fluttered and flipped. Handsome as sin, Luc Martineau appealed on every level.

Unsettled, she tried to tell herself it was no more than a natural physical response to a handsome man. She couldn't afford to get involved with anyone. Not when Seb's future was tied into building up this plantation. Which brought her right back to Luc's odd reaction.

She needed more information about him.

An engine revved loudly on the track below and a single headlight flashed through the palms lining the driveway. A rider gunned the motorbike out of the final curve and screeched to a halt in a spray of gravel at the bottom of the steps. He switched off the engine and sat straddling the bike and grinning up at her.

"Seb! What in heaven's name are you doing on that thing?"

"She's a beauty, isn't she? Needs some body work, but it's the same as Marlon Brando rode in that film we saw in New Orleans."

"What—?"

"You know, Evie. *The Wild One.* We saw it at the movie house when—"

Control spun away as she contemplated Seb's latest recklessness. How was she to deal with a teenage boy bent on seeking out and engaging in the most dangerous activities? "I don't care what Mr Brando rode. What are *you* doing on that bike?"

He kicked a leg over the seat and stood. Shoulders hunched, his mouth tightened and he shoved his hands into his jacket pockets. "I bought it. Or at least I promised the owner I'd get the money to him by the end of the week."

Belligerent as James Dean and as rebellious as Harry. *What can I do?*

"Come on, Evie. I need something to get around on. It's loads cheaper than a car, and I can take you for a ride."

"Where do you expect me to sit? On the fuel tank? There's no pillion seat. No, Seb, you won't be getting me to ride that—that *machine* and neither should you."

"C'mon, Evie. You said you want me to learn from some old geezer. If I've got the bike I can get to work by myself. You won't have to drive me around."

Her anger and annoyance ebbed as Seb twisted her around his little finger. She was such a pushover where he was concerned but motorbikes were so dangerous. "I don't mind driving you. I've just got to get used to the mad road rules here. Whoever thought driving on the right side of the road would be so challenging?"

Seb grinned at her, bounded up the steps and grabbed her hand. "I can help you. It's easy. Just let me get the bike, please? There's more than enough in my trust fund to pay for it."

"I don't think your father would have agreed."

"Dad would have been on that bike and off for a ride like a

shot."

Unavoidably true. Phillip would have loved the rush of speed on land almost as much as he loved flying. How could she keep her nephew safe and still allow him to be his father's son?

Seb raised his free hand to her shoulder and looked her in the eye. "Look, I promise I'll be careful and I won't miss a day with the old man."

"Teenage boys need space to grow."

But it was so dangerous.

"Compromise. It's much better than butting your head against a brick wall."

She drew a shaky breath and swallowed. "We'll see. And Mr Martineau isn't old. He's quite handsome—er, young, in fact. And he's training other young men like you so you see, you'll be able to make friends quickly."

Seb grunted and sidled past her. "What's for dinner? I'm starving."

Laughter bubbled up at the familiar teen complaint. "Typical teenager. You're always hungry, Seb."

"I'm a man and I need feeding." His voice cracked on the last word, somewhat spoiling the effect of his deepening tone. He was a man, or nearly so. Eva knew she had to remember that.

Laughing, she pushed him towards the door. "Dinner. Ten minutes. Go and change."

She leaned against the post at the top of the steps and peered into the darkness. The track Luc had taken was hidden by night, which fell swiftly in Hawaii, unlike the long twilight in England. Would she ever get used to it?

From deep within the palm grove, three notes of birdcall trilled and were carried away on the breeze.

Face raised to the night sky, Eva inhaled deeply. Unfamiliar perfumes twined with the scent of white ginger growing beside the veranda. The garden at Bellerose had always been her refuge.

A garden. She'd start with plumeria and that red hibiscus.

Hope and optimism flowed with her plans and the exotic perfume.

It was all so different from Bellerose, but maybe she could make it work. She *had* to make it work. For both their sakes.

Chapter Three

Luc cradled the hand piece of the phone between his shoulder and ear. Frustration grew with each ring as he folded a slip of paper and tucked it into his wallet. "Come on, Jack. Pick up the damned phone."

"Lyons Realtors. Jack Lyons here." Brisk and business-like, finally his best friend answered.

"Is Benson's sale final or do I have time to negotiate with Eva Abbott?"

"Hello, Luc. I'm fine. You?"

Luc ran his free hand through his hair and leaned against the door frame. "What the hell are you doing?"

"*I'm* having a conversation. People do, you know, at least, normal people do. *You*, on the other hand, are a demanding son of a—"

"Sorry. Look, I'm just a bit—"

"Yeah, you are. Hey, sorry about the deal falling through. I tried to get hold of you at your hotel."

"Annie told me."

"I know what that place means to you, buddy, and I tried to tip it your way, but I got this feeling Benson was looking for any buyer but you."

"Losing this deal will set my community programme back."

"It won't be great for the Tourism Board application either. I could have a word with our lovely new owner and try to negotiate something if you like."

"Look, I just want to find out if Miss Abbott's sale is—"

"Did our lovely heiress give you the brush-off? Is that why you're grumpier than usual this morning?

"Are you nuts? I've got more to worry about than a woman." Luc loved Jack like a brother but sometimes his friend really pissed him off.

"Can't you stand the competition? Anyway, I think she likes me. I rather fancy marrying into money. You can be my best man if you pay up on our bet."

Luc stiffened. "Have you no respect? She's in mourning, Jack. Give her space and give that competitive nature of yours a rest. Besides, vulnerable women aren't your style and she's no good-time girl."

"I knew it. Damn, I thought I'd have time this morning to smooth my way into her good books but you slipped up there last night and played your concerned citizen card, didn't you?"

"Will you stop being an ass for just one minute? The only man she wants right now is her nephew. I offered to train him, same as the other boys. Got it? Now, is the sale *final*?"

"None of your damned business." *Tap, tap, tap.*

Luc heard Jack's trademark pencil hitting the desktop, followed by his heavy expulsion of breath.

"Of course it's final. Why else would she have moved into the place already? Damn it, I tried to contact you at the conference hotel to up your offer to Benson but you never returned my calls."

Luc's stomach clenched. It was only what he'd expected, but hope had reared its two-faced head. He'd deluded himself because he wanted the property so badly; it wasn't Jack's fault. "All those boxes looked like a permanent move. I owe you one."

"You owe me a single malt. Tell you what, if you convince our heiress to sell to you, I'll buy you two bottles."

"Right, like that will happen. Thanks for trying." Luc breathed out an exasperated sigh as he replaced the receiver. It had been worth a shot. He picked up his hat and keys and walked out to the Jeep. No closer to a solution, he started the engine.

What was the right approach to use with Eva to entice her to sell?

Money motivated most women but according to Jack and

Annie, Eva was an heiress. Diamonds and dresses and travel were probably the stuff of everyday life for her. His lip curled as an image of his mother on the arm of her new beau ghosted through his memory. Bedazzled by wealth beyond her wildest dreams, his Louisiana mother had walked out with her oil-rich Texan without a backward glance. Fur coats and monstrous Cadillacs were more important than family. Just like Genevieve Benson. Heartless. The only heart women like them needed was made of solitaire carats.

Despite her outward appearance, Eva Abbott would be the same. How many carats would it take to convince her to sell the plantation to him? And if not money, what else did he have to bargain with?

***

Luc swung the wheel of the Jeep around the last bend of Eva Abbott's driveway and pulled up next to a motorbike in need of panel work. A young man, auburn hair flopping in his eyes, squatted beside the machine at the bottom of the steps. Luc strolled over and examined the bike. "That's a 1950 6T Triumph Thunderbird. Hard to come by in the islands."

"Yeah, and I've got to convince Evie to let me keep it."

Luc held out his hand. "I'm Luc Martineau. You must be Seb."

The young man wiped his hand on an oily rag before shaking hands. "Do you know anything about bikes?"

"A bit. What's the problem?" He hunkered down beside Seb and ran a hand across the dented gas tank. "This doesn't look too bad. I know somewhere you can work on this, tools included."

Excitement lit the teen's face. "Where? Evie might let me keep the bike if I can do the work myself. She's all for being self-sufficient and independent."

The observation fit oddly with Luc's image of an heiress, and he filed it away. "I've a well-stocked machinery shed on my plantation. After you've finished work for the day, you're welcome to make use of the tools."

"*You're* my boss? I thought Evie said you were old. At least"—the teenager shuffled his feet, colour burning up his fair cheeks—"I mean, you don't look that old."

"I'm not quite decrepit, if that's what you mean, son."

Seb stared at the ground beside him and tapped the monkey wrench against his thigh. "Um, do you want Evie?"

Luc folded his arms and clamped his lips together before his brain voiced an automatic *Hell, yeah!* Seb didn't need to know his aunt was the object of Luc's lustful imaginings. "I did come to speak with your aunt. Is she home?"

"Go on in. She's probably—"

"Luc? I mean Mr Martineau, good morning." Eva descended the steps, arms full of scrunched newspapers and a black smudge streaking across her cheek. With her hair pulled back from her face by a fancy clip, her resemblance to young Seb was even more noticeable. "Still unpacking here, I'm afraid. Can I offer you a cup of tea? Or is it Seb you came to talk to?"

"If you have time, I'd like to continue last night's discussion."

"I have time. Seb, take this rubbish to the incinerator and burn it before you spend any more time on that machine." She dumped the pile of papers in his arms before starting back up the steps.

Seb's expression was mulish.

The boy had more to learn than managing a plantation.

Turning his back to Eva, Luc leaned over and quietly addressed the teenager. "Bad idea, son. Woman asks for something, give it to her with a smile." He rested a hand on the motorbike and his voice grew louder for Eva's benefit. "I look forward to seeing this beauty when you've finished doing her up. Reckon maybe your aunt won't object to her when she sees how good she looks."

Understanding flickered into Seb's eyes.

"Go on. Your aunt and I have things to discuss."

Seb loped off with the newspapers and Luc turned to Eva. "Hope you don't mind me dropping in again so soon."

Colour flared under the smudge on her cheek, her fair skin like a beacon marking her change of mood. Abruptly, she turned on her heel and led him to a pair of Adirondack chairs on the veranda and perched on the edge of the furthest seat.

Reminding Miss Evangeline Abbott that she had fallen into his arms last night was a mistake. English roses had thorns and he needed to keep her on his side if he was to convince her to sell him the plantation. And to help her nephew. But the memory of her wide-eyed awareness and slide of her soft, fair skin beneath his hand distracted him.

If his business with her were to succeed, he'd do well to keep his attraction hidden for the time being. Lusting after his English neighbour was secondary to convincing her to sell this place to him.

Unless bedding her helped his cause?

No. After that brief moment in his arms, Eva had clung to her personal space. Friendship and an interest in her nephew's education appeared to be the key.

With a wary eye on her stiff posture, Luc dropped his hat beside the chair, laid his forearms along the chair arms, and sat back.

"We need to talk about Seb joining the training program."

Like flower petals unfurling, she unclasped her hands, half-turned in her seat, and leaned forward. "You'll take him on? I wasn't sure after last night."

Luc relaxed his grip and tried to ease the kink in his neck muscles. The boy was the key. He should have seen that straight away but shock had knocked him out of the ballpark last night.

"Ah, yes. Sorry I left before we had time to talk it through. That's why I called today. My rules for the boys are simple. They turn up every day, on time, pull their weight, and stay out of trouble. No alcohol allowed in their quarters for those who live in, even for the ones who are old enough. It's too tempting for the younger ones."

"Absolutely. Seb's a good lad. I would expect nothing less from him."

"And if he rides over on that bike of his, he can put in a couple of extra hours in the workshop each day fixing it."

Her eyes widened before she narrowed them, shaking her head slowly. "I don't know if I should let him keep it. It's awfully dangerous."

Better tread more carefully. "Have you thought more on what we were talking about last night? About compromise?"

She nodded but her shoulders hunched and she broke eye contact.

"Consider it. Seb keeps the bike if he commits to working hard with me. He'll have to pull his weight and study to earn the reward."

She shook her head again. "I can drive him or he can walk down, can't he? You walked here last night."

"True, but I wouldn't recommend taking the track on foot in the dark."

"But if you can do it—"

"It can be dangerous in the dark. Tell me, does Seb want to be a plantation manager? Is this his choice or yours? It is a huge commitment." There was hope for him to purchase the property if the boy was unwilling to go along with her plans. He watched her closely but she didn't blush with guilt, only became thoughtful.

"I think he's happy. We talked about it a lot before we made the decision to sell up. He rather liked the idea that some of our ancestors had been here before us. It made leaving Bellerose a little less traumatic. Only"—she clasped her hands together and her focus dropped to her tightly interlinked fingers—"I did wonder about the wisdom of investing in a pineapple plantation. Seb has so much to learn but our family solicitor recommended this purchase after—"

She turned to the field of pineapples. Row upon row marched down the slope just visible between the trunks of the palm grove. "How long before they're ready for picking?"

He followed the direction of her eyes. "That particular field, three or four weeks. Benson planted it not long before he fell ill and had to put the place on the market. Second and subsequent crops take fourteen to fifteen months from planting to harvesting but it's not an exact science."

"Do you mean other fields might be ready sooner? How will we know when to pick them?"

Luc frowned. "Good grief, Eva. I knew you were a novice but did you buy this place knowing nothing about pineapple growing?"

She sat ramrod straight and a muscle quivered in her jaw. "We had an ancestor who owned a plantation in the Islands a couple of centuries ago. Besides, with the recommendation of our family solicitor, I worked out a plan with our accountant. It's a good investment. Minor details can be worked out as we go."

An idea blazed to life and took root in his brain. Like a gift from the gods, her inexperience answered his prayer. Self-sufficient and independent. Seb's description of his aunt circled in his mind like a merry-go-round.

All he had to do was enumerate the difficulties of a lone woman and a teenage boy trying to run the plantation. By the time he'd shown her the amount of work and the variety of problems awaiting an amateur grower, Eva Abbott would be only too happy to sell him the property.

If he could find her family plantation, that could tip the balance in his favour.

For a heartbeat or two, he contemplated her vulnerability. She needed him. She needed his knowledge and experience and contacts. And someone *owed* him for stealing his dream. One way or another, he was going to acquire this property but until he figured out the how, he'd play the obliging neighbour.

"I have so much to learn. I don't even know how pineapples are harvested."

Before he knew what he was doing he was out of the chair and raising her to her feet. "Come with me. We'll take a drive and check on the other fields." He offered his arm and led her to the Jeep then headed off towards the closest field. They bounced along the track until, at the highest point, he pulled up and climbed out.

Eva followed him to the nearest row of plants.

He scooped up a handful of dirt and held it out, his thumb breaking apart a clod. "See how red the soil is? It's decomposed volcanic ash. Pineapples love it. You've got over twenty-eight thousand plants in this acre alone."

"Oh, my. That's a lot of plants."

"It is, especially when you factor in they are picked by hand."

"But there's a team here already, isn't there? My solicitor said everything was included in the sale price, and there was an onsite manager although we haven't met him yet. We bought it as a profitable and going concern."

He shook his head and watched her dismay deepen. "Benson managed his own property. Most planters do. And pickers usually move from one plantation to another. Managers look after the booking of them."

She was quiet for several seconds. "So without a manager, I'll have to organize a team until Seb learns where to hire pickers and so on."

"Even if he's a quick learner, it's going to take a couple of years before he knows enough to even begin looking after this place."

Her shoulders slumped and a soft sigh slipped between her lips. "A couple of years? But I thought— Never mind."

"You'll need help. It's not something you can undertake alone."

"Naturally. I'll need to employ an overseer to manage the

place until Seb's able to. Can you recommend anyone?"

"I'll give it some thought." Seeds of doubt sown, he helped her back into the car. They bumped along the track above the fields. Skirting a stand of palms, he pulled up on a bluff. Overlooking the sea, the far edge of her property joined his. Waves crashed on the rocks below creating miniature rainbows.

He turned to her. Hair windswept and cheeks pink from the drive, she looked approachable, not distant. Less the cool heiress and more like the warm, enticing woman he'd held for seconds last night. Distracted by her scent and proximity, he almost forgot why he'd driven to the lookout. Making out wasn't on the menu. He looked towards the horizon and marshalled his errant thoughts.

"I'm curious. Why did you choose to follow in your ancestors' footsteps?"

"It does seem a bit of an odd choice for a pair of Brits like us. Actually, there's a family story that Sebastien le Clerc was a pirate who fell in love with my great, great, however many times removed grandmother, Madeleine, and settled here on a plantation. I'd love to find out which one."

"You bought this property without checking your family history?"

She slipped a glance sideways at him before studiously focusing on the scene in front of them. "It seems like a silly, romantic notion put like that. I should have done more research before making an offer. My solicitor told me about this place as Bellerose was being sold and somehow, it seemed like fate."

"Why didn't you stay on there?"

"Two words—death taxes. On an estate the size of Bellerose, one lot of taxes is difficult, two nearly wiped us out."

"Two?"

"One when my parents were killed in an air raid on London and Bellerose passed to Phillip. The second—"

"—when your brother died. I see." If she'd sunk most of their sales proceeds into the Benson estate, he just had to make

25

sure his offer was too tempting to refuse. *His.* She had his plantation and he was going to get it back.

"I have a proposition for you. A business proposal."

"I'm listening, though I should tell you up front I—I don't have a cash flow yet. I—can't pay you for Seb's training until—"

"You want Seb to learn to manage the plantation but it will take time you don't have. My proposal is to oversee operations on your place and train Seb."

She appeared to consider his offer. Hardly daring to breathe, Luc's chest tightened as he waited for her answer.

"That will be a lot of work. Since I can't pay you, I imagine you have some alternative idea for payment? What do you want in return?"

Several ways of making love to her flashed through his mind. He shut them down and zeroed in on the business.

"A ten percent share of the plantation and first option to buy, should you decide to sell."

Lips parted, Eva's eyes widened then abruptly, she closed her mouth and looked away, a frown wrinkling her forehead.

He should have set up the moment, led into it and given a carefully rehearsed and fully prepared speech. Lord, why hadn't he thought through that half-baked idea before blurting it out?

Because he wanted this property too much not to fight for it. And because, in spite of his disappointment over the sale, he did want to help Eva and Seb. They touched something in him, perhaps some tattered remnant of honour rooted deep within.

"I won't give it away." Hands fisted in her lap, her voice remained calm and steady. "What makes you think I'd want to sell?"

Luck might be with him. She hadn't given him an outright 'No.'

"You retain full control, other than decisions necessary to the efficient operation of the plantation, which would be in my hands. And you gain immediate access to funds through selling me a ten percent share."

"And I can buy back that share from you at anytime?"

Ten percent share in the Benson estate would be enough to convince the Board of the viability of his tourism proposal. Ten percent was a foothold, a starting point for negotiations. It would make his next offer to buy that much easier to accept. He hesitated a fraction too long before answering. "Of course."

"Luc, I'm sure it's very fair, and I appreciate the offer. But this will pass to Seb one day and that's all there is to it. I appreciate you taking him on. Really, I don't expect more."

He breathed in a long, calming breath while his heart slowed to a pace as sluggish as a lava flow. *So close.* She'd come so close to agreeing.

So many things were stacked against Eva succeeding that he only had to bide his time, but he couldn't afford even that delay if he wanted the tourism contract.

My ancestors once owned a plantation here. "You said your family once owned land somewhere in the islands. If we locate it and it's a good prospect, I'd be willing to buy the Benson place so you could buy back your ancestors' property."

Her gaze narrowed on him. "You seem awfully keen on purchasing my land. Why?"

Maybe part of the truth would be enough to satisfy her. "The more land I own, the more boys I can take into the program."

"So your motives are purely philanthropic?"

"In part, yes. Of course it will also generate more income. As a long-term business strategy, I would like to increase my holdings but the important thing right now is to expand the community youth program."

She tipped her head to the side and watched him, assessing and thoughtful. "If not my land, would you look elsewhere?"

He'd wanted Benson's place for so long, the thought of alternatives hadn't crossed his mind. "Eventually. Naturally my preference would be to have further acquisitions nearby. More economical. The arrangement I proposed would be mutually beneficial. Will you consider my proposal?"

"I need time. Let me think about it."

At least she was still open to the idea. For now, it would have to do. "Fair enough. I'll see Seb tomorrow morning. He can start out with the other boys checking ripeness and sugar content. Might as well throw him in the deep end."

"Thank you. I really appreciate it."

He started the engine and reversed until they reached a clearing where he could turn around. As he changed gear and they headed down the track, he glanced over at Eva. Her clear green gaze fixed on him. Was she sizing him up? Truth would always be the best choice with Eva. Truth was, he wanted to get to know his pretty neighbour better. Much better.

Chapter Four

As he drove to Eva's place less than a day after making her the offer, Luc considered his new plan. It was neat, and easy, and so simple he was hopeful that Eva would agree.

Memories of pre-teenage pirate games with Jack had twined with Eva's story of her pirate ancestor and kept him awake into the early hours. Jack had played first mate to his pirate captain as they ran wild on a long-abandoned plantation a few miles' bike ride from home. Could that have been the land owned by Eva's family long ago? Gut instinct might only be hope in disguise but he would work with the idea.

He pulled up and looked over the ripening pineapples. Today, he planned to woo Eva with a lot of charm and the enticement of her romantic family history being real.

The front door opened with a squeak before the screen door pushed wide and Eva stepped through, looking cool and elegant. "Luc. I heard your car. How nice to see you."

He plunged head first into his plan without greeting her. "I've got a surprise for you. Are you game?"

Her face lit up in a smile that lightened the tension knotting his stomach. "I love surprises. What is it?"

"We're going for a ride. Do you have time now?"

"Where to?" She reached inside, and returned a moment later with a broad-brimmed straw hat and sunglasses.

"You'll see." He settled her in the Jeep and climbed in and started the engine. "It's not far from here." Before he spoke again, he negotiated the winding driveway. "By the way, I've organised a team of pickers for you. Lucky to get them at short notice.

"Thanks. That was quick."

"My pleasure. I had to call in a favour but it solves one of your immediate problems." They sat in companionable silence until, as the car rounded a bend, one of the most stunning seascapes on the island opened before them. He'd forgotten how dramatic the view was.

Eva gasped and leaned out of her window for a closer look as Luc eased the Jeep onto a dirt shoulder. "Oh, my. That bay is incredible. It looks large enough for a couple of sailing ships to moor there."

"True. Your pirate ancestor story reminded me of this place. Its name used to be Tallship Bay. Would you like to see more?"

"Yes, please."

Overgrown and long disused, the entrance was difficult to find, but at last he spotted the tamarind tree that he and Jack had climbed when they were young boys. It towered over a riotous profusion of hibiscus and bougainvillea that hedged the northern edge of the estate. He moved aside a sweep of twiggy branches. "Through here. Mind the thorns."

The passage narrowed, and forced her to squeeze past him. Her floral scent teased his nose and her bare arm brushed his chest. Through his shirt, her touch grazed his nipple. He swallowed, resisting the urge to lower his arm, and pull her against him. But getting up close and cosy with his beautiful neighbour wasn't on today's schedule. Convincing her that this might have been her family's land was.

She hesitated, and half-raised her hand before hurrying through the filtered shadows and into the clearing.

He cleared his throat and followed her. "I'd almost forgotten how beautiful it is here."

"Why was it abandoned?"

"Hurricane. Followed by flooding rains and mudslides that carried the old home into the waters of the bay. The slide left this higher section of garden untouched."

**

Flutters of excitement stirred in Eva's stomach. Was it

possible she was standing on Sebastien and Madeline's plantation?

Safe at rest, at home. In the water, by the water, in the garden. The words in Josephine's diary crossed the page like fine gossamer web. Light spidery writing that was almost invisible but she had deciphered it.

Studying the landscape, she pointed out a depression in the upper slope. "Was there a well there?" Josephine had never left New Orleans and her necklace would almost certainly have been hidden there—but Eva's heart beat faster.

In the water, by the water, in the garden.

Luc eyed the depression then strolled over and hunkered down to run a hand across the grassy dip. "I don't remember one, and I doubt as a child I could have left a well unexplored. But this depression looks too regular to be natural. Maybe there was. Why?"

"It reminded me of something." Her gaze strayed back to the bay. "Do we have time to go down to the beach?

Luc nodded, and kept pace with her as they wandered down the hill. "I remember playing pirates here with Jack when we were children. Our ship would be anchored in the bay. One time, we dug under the tamarind tree for a whole afternoon, convinced pirates had hidden their treasure between its roots."

"Are you saying this land belonged to my ancestors?"

"It might have. I don't know but I can imagine your pirate anchoring his ship in this bay."

They stopped on a large, flat-topped boulder and looked at the water. Waves shushed up the sand, and a seabird dipped low into the water before it cleared the waves with a small fish in its beak.

Luc jumped down three feet to the sand, turned and extended both hands to help her climb down. "Shall we?"

Eva hesitated. Brushing against him earlier in the green tunnel, she had experienced a ridiculous desire to cast off caution and continue her accidental touching of his chest. Accepting further contact with her handsome neighbour was not a good idea. The memory of his hands on her body, sliding up her thigh, and curving beside her breast at their first meeting, was all too vivid. She shook her head. "I don't think—"

"I don't bite, Eva."

He waited, hands at the ready while his eyes challenged her to make a small leap of faith. Did he offer courtesy, or seduction? Pleasant and helpful as he'd been, Eva didn't trust him. He wanted her land, perhaps badly enough to pursue her for it. And Luc appealed on a primal level. His body drew hers like a magnet but she was determined to resist. Never again would she be duped by sweet talk.

She edged forward and rested her hands lightly on his shoulders. Muscles bunched as his hands closed around her waist. Effortlessly, he swung her clear of the rock, and leaned back. Corded muscle stood out on his neck as his warm breath played on her bare skin in the V of her blouse. Holding her close, he lowered her to the sand. Breasts grazed solid chest and she feared he would feel her response through her padded bra. Thighs brushed and warmth throbbed beneath her petticoat.

And in his eyes. His head lowered toward her.

Her feet sank into sand, reminding her this was perhaps a scene set for seduction. Dragging in a breath, she pushed away and headed for the water. How was she to keep a cool head around her handsome neighbour? Business came first, not pleasure.

"Eva?" He stopped beside her.

"I've been thinking about your offer. It's generous but, under the circumstances, I can't accept it."

"I know you want to keep the property intact to pass on to Seb. But what if this land belonged to your family? My offer to buy the Benson estate still stands."

"You want more land to expand your operations. Why don't you buy this estate?"

"It's not best practice to separate fields. Besides, wouldn't you like to purchase your ancestors' land? Keep it in the family, especially after having to sell up the manor in England."

Pain lingered in her soul. She had failed her family and dishonoured her name when she'd sold Bellerose. Hawaii was her last chance to redeem herself and build up something worthwhile. Committed to her choice, she would make a go of the larger Benson plantation. Without the distraction Luc Martineau offered.

"I will make my plantation a success. My decision is final."

Chapter Five

Eva stepped away from the oven and stretched. Her back ached all the way from her hips to her neck. She moved the tray she'd taken from the oven to the windowsill to cool. Her arm muscles were like jelly as she beat up the last batch of cookies. After a week of trying to do everything from office manager to cook, exhaustion had become her constant state of being.

"Knock, knock. Can I come in?" Jack Lyons stood in the doorway, casually dressed in a Hawaiian shirt and long shorts. The first time she'd met him his shirt had been bright blue. Now, lurid orange pineapples vied with green palm trees against the red background of his shirt.

"Mr Lyons. I'm sorry I didn't hear you. Come in." Quickly she wiped floury hands on her apron and cleared a space at the table. "Would you like a cold drink?"

"Love one, thanks." He pulled out a chair and sat. "I didn't expect to find the heiress up to her elbows in flour."

"Heiress? Oh, that stupid news article. Were you expecting to find me baking in my tiara?" She placed several freshly cooked biscuits on a plate and slid it toward him.

"Frankly, Miss Abbott, I'm disappointed. I wanted to see that tiara. Or an emerald necklace." He picked up one of her biscuits and bit into it. "But the heiress sure can cook. Delicious."

"Thanks. Did you call in just to compliment me on my cooking?"

"I was in the area and popped in to see how you're doing. I've got a lead on your ancestors' property. You were right about it being on this island but it will take a couple of weeks for copies of the old land deeds to arrive from the capital. I could show you the land. It's not far from here."

"That's kind but I can't see myself having time to spare for a while. There's too much to be done here."

And Eva had already seen the land that she knew in her bones had belonged to her family. She carried a jug to the table and poured icy juice into two glasses before passing one to Jack.

"I see that you've hired pickers but why not a cook, too?"

"Keeping it simple for the time being. And as you observed, I can cook. Mr Martineau gave me a contact who brought his team in as a temporary solution." But she couldn't afford to lurch from one temporary solution to another. She needed a long-term plan. And a manager. Luc's offer was unacceptable, yet ten percent share of the plantation was very reasonable when she considered the workload. A weak and selfish part of her longed to rethink his proposition and hire a cook and manager.

"I'm surprised Luc didn't offer to help out. He's usually the first to lend a hand."

Had she spoken aloud? Flustered by Jack's uncanny pick up on her thoughts, she stammered a rebuttal. "He did. I mean, he offered an arrangement but I—it wasn't one I could agree to."

Jack's eyes narrowed. Slowly, he raised his glass and drank deeply, before he leaned back in his chair. "Of course, you know Luc expected Benson to sell this place to him?"

Luc had intimated as much when he'd offered to take on the day-to-day management. The memory of his odd reaction and abrupt departure the night they met came to mind. Was it possible he'd only heard about the sale from her? Did he blame her because he missed out on the property? Prickles of unease mingled with sweat from the oven's heat and ran down her spine. Was that the reason for his offers of assistance?

"Unlucky for him I made a better offer then."

Jack chuckled and shook his head. "Given the relationship between Benson's daughter and Luc, well— Benson was never going to accept Luc's offer although he led him to believe he had a chance. Luc was very disappointed when he found out you'd sneaked in below his offer and got the place. Almost as bad as Genevieve refusing his marriage proposal."

Her stomach flipped as her image of Luc Martineau took a beating. If she'd understood Jack correctly, Luc was no more than a—a gold digger willing to marry to gain land. No better than Timothy Smythe-Jones when he'd proposed to her, expecting to gain Bellerose along with her hand.

Was it possible Luc's concern for Seb—*and for her*—was not genuine? A sinking feeling settled in the pit of Eva's stomach but she had to know. "You don't mean he asked Benson's daughter to marry him so he could get this plantation?"

Jack shrugged and finished off his drink. He leaned across the table and lowered his voice as though sharing a secret. "He'd do almost anything to get this place. Part of his *grand scheme* you might say."

Eva struggled to breathe around the constriction in her throat. Luc had proposed to Benson's daughter—*to get the plantation?* Then he'd made Eva an offer to manage it for a share, with first right of refusal if she decided to sell. She had almost succumbed to his *kind* offer. Treachery lurked in Luc's offer, not friendship, nor sentimental desire to help her find her family property. Pure revenge sat at the heart of his dealings with her.

Anger surged like a powerful drug through her veins. Forewarned was forearmed. Luc and Timothy, they were obviously tarred with the same brush. She'd build this plantation up on her own if it was the last thing she did. And show Luc Martineau he couldn't buy what he wanted. Or marry to acquire it.

She took a deep breath, seeking an inner calm that had eluded her since he had appeared on her doorstep.

"Since you're here I wonder, do you know of anyone who might take on the manager's position?"

Jack grinned as he got to his feet and pushed the chair in. "I'll ask around. Give me a few days, I'm sure I can find someone."

She forced a stiff smile as she followed him out. "Thanks. I'd appreciate that."

***

Eva lifted another couple of books from the packing box and placed them on the pile beside the slim brown diary. The temptation was too great and she opened it to the page that had caught her attention earlier in the evening. Tracing the curving line on the sketch with the tip of her forefinger, she wondered, might this be the answer to their financial difficulties?

An engine roared to a halt on the gravel drive. She dropped the book into her lap and turned her head to listen. A few moments later, heavy boots clattered up the front steps followed by the crash of the screen door.

"Seb? Is that you?"

She stretched and sat back on her heels. The diary slid to the floor. She retrieved it and set it on the table out of harm's way.

Since her chat about not becoming too familiar with their neighbour or taking advantage of his *kind* offer, Seb had been at work all day and then away half the night. He'd refused to say where he'd been. More mulish than both his uncle and his father combined, after that fiasco of a conversation she hadn't been able to forbid him the motorbike. She cocked her head and waited.

"Seb? I'm in the library."

Scuffling sounds by the front door were followed by two heavy thumps before soft footfalls approached. At least he'd taken his boots off at the door.

"Hi, Evie. What's for dinner?" Spikes of sweaty hair stood out from his head like porcupine quills and a streak of oil marked his forehead. Covered in grease, his T-shirt was hardly fit for the ragbag and his jeans looked like they'd stand up without him.

"What have you been doing?"

Hands shoved deep in his pockets, he lounged against the doorframe. "Fiddling with my bike. Why did you bring this junk from home? Looks like you brought the entire library with you."

37

Her throat constricted as she skimmed familiar covers of books that marked various stages of her life. "This is all that's left of Bellerose."

All that's left of home.

"Mouldy leather and dusty pages. Don't suppose there's a treasure map hidden in this lot?" Seb picked up the nearest book. Small and covered in soft, dark brown leather, the spine had darkened with age and the touch of many hands. Including hers. A fine trace of silver marked the edge of letters etched into the front—*JD, Josephine Dubois.*

She watched him flip through several pages. Household accounts filled the early section and she doubted he saw more than columns of numbers. The really interesting entries started further in, descriptions that made her cheeks burn even as they compelled her to read on. Since she had arrived here, the entries had made her think the touch of Luc's hands, his hard body pressed against hers. What would it be like to share with him the things Josephine and her lover, Ivan had shared?

Seb flicked over a couple more pages. Amid details of what must have been a torrid love affair with the Russian fur trader was a page he might consider as good as a treasure map. Uncomfortable with the idea of him reading Josephine's account of her trysts with her lover, Eva reached for the diary and gently eased it out of his hands.

"Evie? You've got a funny look on your face. What is it?"

"I found something, a drawing." She skipped over several pages until she found the sketch. Indecision warred within her.

"Of a treasure map? Please tell me we're going to be rich." Bright-eyed with enthusiasm for the first time in days, his sullen mood disappeared in an instant.

Young and still grieving for his father, Seb needed something exciting. An adventure, or the promise of one, could divert his thoughts.

"It's not a map but it is valuable, maybe priceless. See."

Holding the diary open, she gave the book back to him. "Emeralds and diamonds worth a tsar's ransom."

He dropped into the nearest chair and studied the page, flicking backwards and forwards and coming back to the sketch. "Where do we dig? Is it here in Hawaii? Is that why we came here?"

Oh, to have the enthusiasm and resilience of youth. She smiled at his exuberance. Her own heart had certainly beat faster when she'd realized the fabulous piece had belonged to her ancestress. "I've no idea, but I'm going to read more of Josephine's diary. There could be clues to the whereabouts of the necklace."

"Imagine what we could do with the money."

"I *imagine* it stayed in New Orleans."

"Why there? Wouldn't it be at Bellerose or here in Hawaii?" He cast her a narrow-eyed, considering look. "Is ours the plantation? Is that why we bought it? But didn't you and Luc visit an abandoned estate at Tallship Bay? I thought—"

"I don't know where our pirate and his bride lived. What I do know is that Josephine, our many times removed great-aunt, lived in New Orleans. When we were invited to that dinner party, a photographer took my photo in front of her portrait." She passed a newspaper photo to him.

He pored over the photo. If only he gave half as much attention to the plantation, their success would be guaranteed. "That necklace she's wearing—it's the same as the sketch!"

"Surely if the necklace still exists…"

Seb held the newspaper photo and the diary up side by side, his gaze shifting between the two. "Why wouldn't it?"

"Expensive pieces like that were often broken up and sold off as individual stones. I even wondered if the single emerald pendant I inherited from my mother might be a remnant of this necklace. Look"—she turned a page and pointed to a description—"she wrote that there were twenty-eight stones. I wouldn't be surprised if one of our ancestors needed money and sold off some of the gems. I expect they would have paid for Bellerose several times over."

"What if they didn't? What if it's just waiting for us to find it? Maybe Luc can help us discover the pirate's plantation. It could be there. We have to find that necklace. It's better than treasure."

"How so?"

He grinned. "You don't have to dig a big hole to hide a necklace."

***

Eva pushed open the screen door and stepped onto the wide veranda. Tropical night flowers perfumed the air but as the sun rose above the treeline, their scent was overtaken by the sweet smell of pineapple as the rising sun warmed the fields. For now, she took a few moments to relax in the solitude of early morning.

Seb's motorbike stood like a sentinel guarding the steps. It gleamed like a new shilling and she squinted into the brightness. Had he painted it? She strolled down the steps to the bike and bent down to examine the fuel tank. Dents and scrapes had been machined into a smooth surface, which now shone under a new coat of paint. Detailing work looked almost professional, aside from one slightly wonky corner cut. She traced the line of blue stripe on silver metal. Could he have achieved this level of work without access to a workshop?

Surely he wouldn't go behind her back? Not after she had forbidden him to impose further on his boss. But the memory of her brothers sneaking out to do exactly the thing they'd been told not to ghosted through her memory.

"Oh, Seb." Thoughts of how that discussion would go tied her in knots and she pressed her hands against her stomach. With a sigh, she turned to march up the steps.

"Missus." Amoka, the hired man in charge of her pickers, moved out of the shadows and strolled to the bottom of the steps. Thumbs hitched into the tabs of his trousers, he looked her up and down. "My team's waiting. You gonna pay us now?"

Amoka's attitude smacked of disrespect and something more disturbing. Menacing, even. She gripped the wooden upright. "Pay you? But you haven't finished picking." Until the crop payments went into her account, she had barely enough to cover the household accounts. "What about the rest of the crop? You have to finish picking that field first."

"No more. We got another job. You pay us now." He stepped closer, crowding her. Stale cigarette smoke and sweat wafted from his clothes and she swallowed, trying to breathe through her mouth.

Dealing with hired hands wasn't as simple as dealing with family retainers. She raised her chin and stood firm and tall. *Look confident, look him in the eye, and demand he finish the job.* "When you've finished this job, then I will pay you and your team."

He edged closer.

Her stomach clenched with fear and roiled at his stale smell.

Unable to tear her gaze from Amoka, Eva prayed for help.

A second male voice joined their conversation. "End of job you get paid. Not before. Those are rules." The heavily accented voice came from beside the garden at the side of the house.

With a careful step away from Amoka, Eva glanced sideways. Black-bearded and arms folded across a massive chest, a heavyset man sauntered over and stood next to Amoka, his black eyes boring into the picker. He was an intimidating figure but beneath his calm exterior Eva sensed a dark menace.

"You heard boss lady. Finish picking, pay after."

Amoka stiffened, his hands fisting at his sides. "Who you telling what to do? You not boss man."

"You not take order from boss lady, you not get work anywhere. Me, I make sure of this. Now, finish picking like she told you to do." He stepped into Amoka's personal space and stared him down.

The picker dropped his gaze. Hands dug in his pockets and muttering, he scuffed the earth with one bare foot then turned and slouched away.

The Russian—Eva now recognized his accent—looked at her, his eyes shadowed beneath bushy eyebrows and the brim of his hat. "Overseeing is not work for women."

Right now, Eva was prepared to agree with him. "Thank you for your help. Did Mr Lyons send you?"

He nodded and bowed stiffly as though unused to the action. "I am Stefan Lutchenko. You need me. I work here now."

"Well, yes, I do need you and I'm delighted Mr Lyons was so quick in finding a manager for me. Come in, please."

Pleased with Jack's quick assistance, she led Lutchenko into the library before she remembered her interrupted unpacking still lay strewn across the floor. Mumbling an apology, she hurried to clear the armchair. "Would you like a cool drink?"

He shook his head and sat. "*Nyet*. I will take coffee."

"I won't be long. Please make yourself comfortable."

She measured the beans and prepared the pot and two cups on a tray. Should she have asked to see his references or spoken to Jack before hiring Stefan Lutchenko? Like she had enough applicants for the position to be worrying about that. If Jack Lyons sent him, that should be good enough.

Frustrating as it was to have to rely on a man, she had acquired a manager and Luc Martineau wouldn't be making another offer to buy anytime soon. They didn't need him or his attempted seduction, and her plantation would be in safe hands.

After making the coffee, Eva carried the tray into the library and placed it on a central table. Sitting on the nearest chair, she lifted the coffee pot and poured, savouring the aroma. "Do you take sugar and cream, Mr Lutchenko?"

He stood by the window, angling a framed photo to the light. Bushy brows were tightly knit and his mouth was a mere slash between beard and moustache. He nodded and turned a sharp gaze on her. "Black only, thank you. This very pretty picture. Is this your necklace in painting?"

"Good gracious, no."

"But you wear emerald necklace in photo?"

"Inherited from my mother. It's just a single emerald, nothing like the splendour of the piece in the painting. Nobody knows where that one is or if it even still exists as a complete piece. A photographer from one of the New Orleans papers asked me to pose for a photo."

"Is very beautiful picture." He replaced the frame and took the cup she offered. "You want I should start today? You have maybe twenty-five thousand plants to harvest in next field and field hands need strong man to supervise. Me. I help you."

She picked up her cup. Coffee slopped into the saucer. It seemed the confrontation with Amoka had shaken her up more than she realized. "Indeed they do and thanks again. You arrived just in time."

"I came immediately. You have place for me to sleep? Is there room behind sheds, maybe?"

Stefan Lutchenko was her black-bearded angel. Having this man who had already faced down the picker nearby might be useful. "There is a room off the back shed that you're welcome to have. You can move into it this evening."

Chapter Six

Luc bounded up the steps of Eva's house. Despite his best intentions, he couldn't wait another day to see her. The deadline for the Tourism Board contract loomed and she had rejected his offer to buy. But she had not denied the attraction that simmered between them. The cool English rose hadn't been able to disguise her response to him.

He would use Seb's progress to justify his visit. It was high time she received a personal report from the boss. The boy had proven to be a good worker and a quick learner, although he was evasive when Luc enquired about his aunt.

Will she be wearing those shorts again today? His groin tightened in anticipation as he relived the moments holding her in his arms. The memory had fuelled several lusty dreams and a number of cold showers. After he concluded the purchase of her property, which he would now that Jack had confirmed the location of her pirate ancestor's land, an affair with the delectable Eva would be very pleasant. Convincing her to agree was just a matter of finding the right button to press.

Luc knocked on the screen door, took his hat off, and ran a hand over his hair.

Eva appeared on the other side of the screen. She wore a pair of blue shorts and a blouse knotted below her breasts. The knot nestled below a valley he'd have given anything to dive into and left a band of soft skin bare above her shorts. He sucked in a lungful of air as his good manners headed south, along with every spare ounce of blood. He grinned at her. "Hi there."

Arms folded, Eva made no move to open the door.

Fiddling with the brim of his hat, he kept his eyes on her face and not on the luscious curve of hip and sweep of thigh. Or the creamy swell of breasts in the V of her blouse. His groin had taken control of his brain. He grabbed the first opening gambit he thought of. "How've you settled in? Got everything you need?"

"What are you doing here, Mr Martineau?"

He'd been so besotted seeing her in another pair of cute shorts that showed off plenty of leg he'd missed her chilly tones and the lack of warmth in her eyes. Like a bucket of cold water, her frosty reception finally hit him. Was she unhappy because Seb had spent so much time working on his bike at Luc's? "*Mister* Martineau? What happened to Luc?"

She shrugged. "I couldn't say where he's gone."

Something had definitely riled her and he needed to sort it out. "May I come in? I thought you'd like to know how Seb's doing and I've good news about your search."

She stiffened, then pressed her lips together and opened the screen door. "There is something I want to ask you."

Her tone would freeze beer but before he could ask what the problem was, she turned on her heel and marched down the hall to the library.

Eva hadn't struck him as the mercurial type but today there was no hint of warmth or softness in her demeanour.

She gestured to the armchair. "Please take a seat."

He sat and dropped his hat beside the chair. "I hope it hasn't been too lonely for you without Seb?"

She moved behind the sofa and leaned on its back, her body straight and tense. Dark smudges he hadn't noticed earlier highlighted her eyes. "Lonely doesn't come into it. I've had my hands full until this morning."

He sat back and observed her. *Ah, that's what's wrong; she's tired and overworked without Seb's help.* Confident he now had a handle on what had upset her, he launched into his progress report. "He's fitting in well. He's a hard worker and the other boys love helping him with his bike in the evenings. I'm glad you decided to loosen the reins. That bike means a lot to him."

Her gaze pinned him. "The bike, he can keep. What I will

not tolerate is you attempting to insinuate your way into our plantation, either by trickery or manipulating a vulnerable young man."

A full-on verbal assault was the last reaction he expected from Eva. Confused, he rose and moved towards her. "Whoa, there. What are you talking about? What manipulation and trickery?"

"Did you think I'd accept you encouraging Seb to defy me?"

He raced through his memory of conversations with the boy over the past few days. Nothing that could be called manipulation in anyone's book. "What has he done? I'll speak to him if he's causing you problems but I haven't encouraged him in anything other than hard work. Look, what's this about?"

She relaxed her fierce grip on the back of the sofa and tipped her head to the side. "My note explained our situation. I thought it was perfectly clear."

"I haven't received any note. What situation? What's changed?"

"You didn't get my note?" A hint of uncertainty crept into her voice but suspicion lingered in the narrow-eyed look she cast him. "We can't pay for your help so I forbade Seb to accept anything more than basic instruction. I will find a way to pay you for that too once—"

He held up a hand to stem her flow of words. "Why? What brought this on?"

"Thankfully Mr Lyons put me straight. When were you going to tell me that you'd bid for this property?"

"Jack told you?" His friend must be really taken with Eva to have shafted him like that. But what had he told her? An offer on the land wasn't that big a deal and she'd won the property.

"Yes, he did and it's nice to know there are some *gentlemen* on the Island." Haughty green eyes challenged him to disagree. Like Genevieve, Eva considered him not good enough.

Not a gentleman and not wealthy enough to tempt even a down-on-her-luck heiress. Anger began a slow burn in his gut. As usual, it was always about money.

Luc's last telephone conversation with Jack ran through his memory and he swallowed the retort that had sprung to his lips.

So much for client confidentiality. "Yes, I did offer to buy it from Benson. I thought you understood that from our chat when you asked if I'd consider an alternative to this place. And I'll offer you the same amount right now if you want to sell."

"Was that before or after his daughter refused your proposal?"

"Hell's bells." Heat ran up his neck and face as he clamped his jaw shut. Knots formed in his stomach. "My personal life is none of your business."

"Puts a different perspective on your *offer*." She leaned forward, eyeing him as though he was a snake in her English garden. "I'm not a fool, nor some starry-eyed young thing without two thoughts to rub together."

"I never thought you a fool but whatever Jack told you, you've misunderstood."

"He was quite clear. So, what are you going to do now? Propose to me? I'll save you the effort. You'll never get hold of my land through wooing me."

"You've got it wrong, and you're wrong about me."

"And did I misunderstand the intent of that cleared track linking your bottom field with mine? That thin line of trees barely masks it."

Damn. He'd jumped the gun giving Samuel the order to clear it the day he arrived home. The boys' excitement at the purchase news had spurred their efforts and, by the time he'd called a halt, they were all but through to Eva's land.

There was no point prolonging the visit. Eva was obviously not of a mind to sell to him today and perhaps not ever. But he wouldn't let Seb suffer any fallout. Luc picked up his hat and moved to the door. "Don't take it out on Seb because you can't see what Jack is trying to do."

"And that would be—?"

"Make brownie points with you. When you've accepted what compels him to behave that way, you know where to find me. Down the track, first house on the right. I'll leave the offer on the table for one week. After that—"

"Don't hold your breath waiting for me, Mr Martineau."

He slapped his hat on and strode out of the house. *Lord, save me from all green-eyed women. And look out, Jack when I next meet you.*

Two hours later, scrunched paper littered the floor around the bin, testimony of his latest attempt at reorganizing his finance to secure the contract. Why had he thought Eva was any different to Genevieve? He conceded she had a point about the track linking their properties—it looked premeditated and arrogant on his part— but how dare she look down her aristocratic nose at him? So much for the attraction he'd imagined at Tallship Bay. Women were all the same and he'd best not forget it.

***

Seb sat across the kitchen table, shovelling fruit pie into his mouth. "This is good," he mumbled around a mouthful. He'd polished off two helpings of the main course and looked ready to do the same with dessert.

Eva picked half-heartedly at her food. All day, she'd debated what to do about Seb and the training he needed if he was to run their plantation one day.

Luc confused her. On the one hand, he was training Seb for free and had organized a picking team for her plantation. But the path cleared between their properties suggested an underhanded motive that gave his assistance a more self-serving interpretation. His desire for her property and the implications of his proposal to Benson's daughter showed he was not to be trusted.

She pushed her plate away and interlaced her fingers. "I

want to talk to you about Mr Martineau.'"

Seb's spoon stopped halfway to his mouth and he looked at her as though she'd proposed sending him to the moon. "What about him?"

"Honestly, how long did you think you could get away with deceiving me?"

His spoon clattered into his bowl. "You know? How?"

"He came to tell me how well you've been doing and about your work on your bike. I must admit I was surprised when he showed up. Seems he didn't receive the note I sent with you."

Seb pushed away from the table, paced to the end of the dining room and spun around to face her. "It wasn't fair setting me up with him and the boys then telling me I couldn't use his workshop. He's been great. And he offered his workshop for free, and Acky and Moe have been helping me and—"

She held up a hand to stem the flow of words. "I get the picture. You like it there, don't you?"

He nodded.

"I need to know I can trust you, Seb. I won't stop you from going to Luc's workshop after work"—his eyes widened and a grin replaced the frown as she spoke—"but I have to be able to depend on you. Can I trust you to tell me everything from now on?"

Like a streak of lightning he raced around the table and folded her in a bear hug. Eva's chin bumped against his shoulder and she looked up at her nephew. When had he grown so tall?

"I promise. Thanks. From now on, no goofing off and no secrets. I'm the man of the house and I'm going to make you proud of me. Just you wait and see."

She stroked his cheek, feeling fuzz beneath her fingers. "I'm already proud of you."

He shuffled his feet and pink coloured his cheeks as he backed away. "I've got study to do. Better get on with it."

"Study?" Since when had Seb enjoyed studying?

"Luc gave me one of his farming books. I'm supposed to

read up on harvesting techniques." He grabbed a handful of biscuits from the plate, tossed her a cheeky grin and ducked through the doorway.

Man of the house indeed. He was growing more like Phillip every day.

***

Eva woke with a start and sat up. Fragments of a nightmare swirled in her memory. Sheets tangled around her legs and strands of hair covered her eyes. With shaking hands, she swiped them clear and pushed the top sheet back. Heart thudding, she swung her legs over the side of her bed and stood. Moonlight flooded through the window, so bright she could almost read by its light. Was that what had woken her?

Fuzzyheaded, she padded to the kitchen for a drink of water. Enough light from the moon lit the room and she left the lights off. She filled her glass at the tap and drank deeply then carried the glass to the window. Silver and black shadows coloured fields of spiky leaved plants beyond the palm grove. Closer to the house a movement caught her eye and a darker shadow slipped through the gap between two hibiscus bushes.

She lowered the glass and peered into the garden. Was there someone out there or was it a remnant of her disturbed sleep?

But she was sure it had looked like a man. The confrontation with Amoka sprang to mind and her muscles froze at the memory of the menace in his expression. All day it had never been far from her thoughts and now it appeared to have invaded her sleep.

Shivers ran down her spine and Eva wrapped her arms across her waist. She checked the lock on the kitchen window and back door and tiptoed down the hall. A floorboard creaked under her foot and she winced. Several heartbeats later, she moistened her lips and moved on to the library.

A gentle breeze caressed her heated skin and teased her nose with the scent of white ginger. Curtains fluttered. The middle window was open.

She edged around several piles of books and stubbed a toe on the table leg. Biting back the cry that hovered on her lips, she felt for the switch of the lamp beside her and flicked it on. A tower of novels still leaned toward the bookcase and three piles of paper lay partially sorted from this morning's half-hearted efforts.

As she crossed to the window, her foot slipped on a piece of paper. Face down on the wooden boards, half under a chair, lay the newspaper photo. As she picked it up, her hand brushed the flapping curtain and a whiff of stale smoke assailed her nose. She lifted the curtain and sniffed. There was no mistaking the odour.

Neither she nor Seb smoked, and the stink of stale smoke and unwashed clothes had almost made her gag when Amoka had crowded her.

Someone had been in here! *Amoka?*

Chest tight, she darted a glance into the shadowy corners, straining to hear if anyone was still outside. Her papers were of little value and even less interest to anyone other than Seb and her. There were several valuable collections of books waiting to be unpacked but the boxes were untouched. What had the intruder been looking for?

Eva raised her hand to rub her eyes. Faint smoke stench clung to her fingers. She shuddered and peered at the newspaper cutting. Had it simply blown onto the floor?

All she could recollect of her nightmare was an emerald necklace that grew larger and heavier around her neck until it dragged her down. Was the photo or the reference to the necklace important to someone? Had she missed something in the diary? Seb had come in, she'd shown him the sketch in Josephine's diary, and they'd joked about finding the emerald necklace and getting rich. Then she'd shown him the photo. *Diary—photo—*she glanced at the side table where she'd placed Josephine's book—

Where was Josephine's diary? She dropped to her knees and peered under the chair.

"Who's there? I know you're there. Show yourself." Deep-voiced, Seb sounded like a man.

Eva sat back on her heels then pushed to her feet. "Seb?"

Seb stood just inside the room, hair standing up in spikes, clutching his cricket bat. His mouth fell open as he looked at her. "Evie? What were you doing down there? I thought someone was in the house."

"I think there was someone in here. That window was open and I found this on the floor below it. Oh, Seb, I think they've stolen Josephine's diary. It was right here." She held out the newspaper clipping and touched the side table as though the book might magically reappear.

Seb lowered the cricket bat and rubbed a hand across the back of his neck as embarrassment crossed his face. "The diary is in my room. I just wanted to see if Josephine left any clues about where she hid the necklace."

"You've got it? In your bedroom?" Tears pricked her eyes and she wrapped her arms around his neck. "Oh, thank goodness. I thought we'd lost it."

Awkwardly, her nephew patted her back. "I'm sorry, Evie. Guess I got carried away with the idea of finding treasure. I should have asked you for permission."

"Just as well you took it. Maybe that's what the intruder wanted, though how anyone would know about it is beyond me. So, did you find any clues in the diary?"

Seb's cheeks turned a fiery red and he avoided her eyes. "No."

Eva drew in a deep breath, aware of what he'd been reading and completely out of her depth. What could a maiden aunt say about sex to her teenage nephew? "Perhaps we should retrieve it from your room and find a better hiding place?"

Chapter Seven

Quicker than the trip by road, the path to Luc's home climbed steeply behind Eva's house until it fell gradually on Luc's side of the ridge, before meandering through a dense grove of palms and down past sloping fields.

Eva sat on a fallen trunk beside the path and wiped her forearm across her brow. As she caught her breath, the sweet, heavy perfume of ripening pineapples insinuated its way into her consciousness.

Somewhere ahead lay Luc's home. Luc hadn't received her note so he hadn't known of her request regarding Seb. Her nephew liked Luc, and the company of the young males in Luc's program was helping him get past his grief. An apology was appropriate.

And necessary. She might not trust Luc's motives, but she would give him the benefit of the doubt when it came to understanding young men. For Seb's sake.

And for her own?

She preferred not to dwell on the emotions induced by proximity to Luc. Steeling her resolve against an inconvenient attraction, she rose to her feet and marched down the path.

As she rounded a bend into open space, a welcome breeze cooled her warm cheeks and the tang of salt air and a view of sunlit sand greeted her. Above her, built into a gentle slope, Luc's house perched on a bluff overlooking the sea.

Lush gardens of bird of paradise and yellow hibiscus vied with elephant ear plants below a wide, shady veranda. Yellows, oranges and greens wrapped around a house of soft grey stone walls, teak trim and shutters. The single story dwelling nestled stately as a queen in the middle of a tropical paradise.

"It's beautiful," she whispered.

"Eva? What are you doing here?"

Luc's voice sounded close behind her left shoulder and her heartbeat kicked up several notches. She turned quickly and her sandal caught in a gnarled root. Arms flailing, she fell. Luc grabbed her wrist, and an arm like an iron band wrapped around her waist and hauled her up close and personal. For the second time in as many weeks, she was breathless in Luc Martineau's arms.

This was a habit she needed to break...and fast.

Eva drew a deep breath and looked up into his eyes. Shadowed by the brim of his hat, flecks of amber highlighted deep wells of chocolate-brown.

"Do you always sneak up on people?" With a jolt, she realized she had wrapped one arm around his neck while the other was pressed against his chest, just over his heart, which thudded strongly beneath her fingers.

His grip on her wrist shifted and his thumb traced a path over the back of her hand. "Do you always throw yourself into men's arms?"

"I don't throw myself."

"So it's just mine you fall into?"

"I tripped." Her voice squeaked and she cleared her throat. "And you'd be the *last* man I'd throw myself at."

Yet why would he believe her when her heart pounded as though she'd run a sub four-minute mile? He must feel it when each breath she took pressed her breasts against his chest. Heat flared between them and awareness blocked out everything but him.

"Seeing you're in my arms, am I to assume we're the last two people on Earth?"

"Not even then, Mr Martineau."

He gave a mirthless laugh but made no move to release her. "Oh, but I think we are, *Miss* Abbott. Here, in my little patch of paradise, there is no one else."

She knew if he released her, she would spin into orbit

around him, unable to escape the force of his attraction. He was the reason she'd walked over, not Sebastian, nor even the break-in. It was crazy and ridiculous and she didn't even like him.

But she wanted him.

She ran her tongue over her top lip. "Um, you can let me go now."

His gaze roamed her face, lingered on her lips. "I like to keep my enemies close."

Breathless, she stammered, "I'm not your enemy."

"Then if you're not my enemy and you're not my friend, what are you?"

"Too close. Please, let me go."

He eased his hold from her waist and she staggered back. Concern flashed across his face as he caught her elbows and steadied her. "Perhaps you should sit. You appear to be shaken by your fall."

She shook her head and straightened her shoulders. If only it was the fall that had shaken her. "I'm fine, thank you."

"Why are you snooping around only a day after you gave me my marching orders? I thought I was the last person you wanted to see."

She darted a glance at his face then looked at the ground. "Seb…"

"Ah, yes, you still need me to train Seb. So you'll put up with talking to me while I'm useful." He released her as though her skin burned him and shoved his hands into his pockets. Jaw clenched, he turned away. "How does it feel to play the martyr, Eva? Does it make you feel virtuous?"

She caught her lower lip, aware of the irony. Virtue didn't come into it. Just the ridiculous sense of security Luc's arms gave her. She shook her head. Her safe place couldn't be in his arms. "I came to apologize. You were right. I shouldn't have said what I did to you."

He leaned against a tree, pushed his hat back with a thumb

and surveyed her. "Big of you."

He wasn't going to make this easy for her. And why should he? What she'd said was inexcusable. "If you'll have him, Seb would love to continue working with you, and—I wanted to thank you for allowing him to fix his bike."

"Seb is welcome here anytime. I don't go back on my word."

"But I'm not. Is that it?" She straightened her shoulders, tipped her chin up and met his gaze. "I guess I deserve that. Thank you for—"

"Of course that's not what I meant." He took off his hat and ran a hand through his hair. Wild disarray suited him, like he'd just gotten out of bed.

Her fingers itched to plunge into the dark waves but fantasy didn't change the fact he wanted her land. Why did he get under her skin so much? "You have a beautiful home."

He slapped his hat against his thigh and met her gaze. "Look, we're neighbours now and Seb is going to be here every day. Shall we at least try to get on better? Truce?"

A truce with Luc meant learning to trust him a little and keeping a rein on her emotional response to him. It would be difficult under the best of circumstances and they had got off on the wrong foot but what choice did she have? She held out her hand. "Truce."

His hand enveloped hers, warm and strong, and extended in guarded friendship. Friendship? It was a beginning, as long as she stopped saying outrageous things to him. If only she could stop wanting the safe feeling his arms gave her, maybe they could be friends. "Good, well, I'm glad that's sorted. I should head back home."

"Why don't you come up to the house, have a drink and then I'll drive you back."

"I should be getting back. Seb—"

"—is working and won't notice where you are." He tipped

his head to one side and scanned her face as though weighing up an important decision. "Have dinner with me? Tomorrow night at the club?"

Yes. Oh, yes. An evening with Luc, maybe dancing in his arms. Then what? Was she strong enough to resist what would surely follow? "I can't. Really, I should be going."

His gaze narrowed on her face and she squirmed uncomfortably.

Heat pooled low in her belly and her bodice tightened, constricting her breathing. Where was her famous ice queen poise when she needed it? It had worked on Timothy Smythe-Jones. *Little Miss Frigidaire* he'd labelled her to his Oxford set.

"Are you afraid to be seen in my company?"

She was afraid. Of Luc and the way he made her feel when he was near. She didn't want to feel like that—exposed and vulnerable. Like she wanted to crawl into his skin with him.

But she couldn't fail to notice the tension in his tone and expression. Had her refusal offended him or was his pride stinging him? "I thought we agreed to a truce."

"And you're avoiding the question. Forget it." His jaw tightened and he stepped away.

Before she realized it, her hand reached for his forearm. "No. I'm—I haven't been out since Phillip…since he died. I'm not afraid of—" She sucked in a breath at the lie.

"Eva? What is it?"

Concern coloured his tone and she thought of how much better she felt when Luc was near. Aside from his offer to buy her land, which had been made up front, his presence made her feel better than she had since Phillip's death. She needed that feeling to last a little longer. "I will take you up on that drink, Luc. I—need to tell you something."

Wordlessly, he took her arm and led her up to the house. They crossed the wide veranda and entered a high-ceilinged reception room. Teak doors and beams contrasted with white walls and carved furniture. He seated her on a rattan chair opposite a picture window that framed a view of the sea. "Would you like a whiskey or juice?"

She raised an eyebrow at him. "Isn't it a bit early in the day for hard liquor?"

"I wasn't sure if you needed some Dutch courage." He poured two glasses of juice, handed one to her, and then sat in the single chair beside her. "So, what do you need to tell me?"

"Last night we had an intruder."

"An intruder? Why didn't you phone me?" He sat forward and the intensity of his scrutiny warmed her, like a protective blanket.

"I'm fine, thank you. I thought I'd had a silly dream but a window was open in the library and a—paper had been folded as though someone was taking it with them but dropped it."

"You didn't see him then?"

Eva shook her head. "I smelled smoke on the curtains this morning." Amoka. It had to be Amoka.

"Was anything taken?"

"Well, that's just it. I think he was looking for a particular something and didn't find it."

"What?"

She'd said too much already. "Look, I don't want to burden you with my nonsense. I just thought you should know, so you can take precautions."

Piercing dark eyes assessed her. "There's something you're not telling me."

**

Eva handed Luc the photo and perched on the edge of her office desk. He had insisted on seeing the library first, and he had discovered footprints along with an unusual black cigarette butt beneath the library window. She hadn't thought to look there.

"You think the intruder was taking this photo? But why? It doesn't make sense."

"I know. But it's the only thing that was out of place and I didn't fold it."

"You said the window was open. Maybe the paper blew down from wherever you'd left it and he stepped on it on his way out. It could be that simple. Unless you have a reason for thinking this photo means something to someone." He examined the photo again and held it up beside her face. "There's a strong resemblance to the woman in the portrait, as well as the red hair. Are you related to her?"

"She was my ancestor, Josephine Dubois. Back in the late eighteenth century, she married a wealthy merchant and moved to New Orleans where that portrait was painted. Her diary records her marriage and—other people she knew." Eva could feel heat creeping up her cheeks. Josephine had *known* Ivan all too well. The memory of some of her entries about her lover elicited a tingly sensation in Eva's stomach. Tingles that spread lower when she looked at Luc. To love someone as Josephine loved Ivan must have been heaven. And hell when she lost him.

"Do you have her diary?"

"Yes."

"Does she talk about the necklace?"

"She sketched and described it. I think it may have been a gift."

"Her husband must have been a very wealthy merchant to afford such a piece."

"I don't think he gave it to her." She cleared her throat. "I think it was a gift from her lover."

Luc's eyebrows rose and he whistled long and low. "Some lover's gift. It looks like a piece fit for a queen. Who was he, this lover?"

"Josephine only referred to him as Ivan. I assume he was Russian by his name."

"So a Russian lover gave your great, great-aunt an emerald and diamond necklace and now, in 1960, this photo is the only thing out of place after a break in. Tenuous link at best, don't you think? Is your family connection to this portrait widely known?" He laid the photo on the desk between them.

"The newspaper did include a paragraph in their article about it. And the local paper here picked up the story when we arrived, although they made a lot of factual errors in their report." Including that heiress label. "But that portrait was painted almost two centuries ago. Why would anyone think we know anything about it now?"

He shrugged. "I don't know. Frankly, as a theory it seems rather farfetched. Look, the break in was probably a one-time incident, opportunistic and nothing more, but I can send over a gun if that would make you feel more secure. I heard you've acquired a manager. I can speak to him if you like, find out if he saw or heard anything."

Luc's calm common sense restored her perspective and his logical approach inspired trust. "I'll talk to Stefan later. I have my father's service pistol. I would have thought of that earlier but I haven't finished unpacking."

"Do you know how to use it?"

"No. Phil showed me how to clean it but I've never wanted to fire it. I hope to God I never have to."

"If you like, I can check it for you now. Have you got it handy?"

Eva nodded and opened the cupboard beneath her father's desk. She ran her fingers over his initials inlaid in the top. Carefully, she placed it on the desk, lifted the lid and removed the pistol. Two-handed, she offered it to Luc.

He tested the weight and checked the sight, opened it and checked the chambers. "It's a fine piece. Would you like a lesson after you've cleaned it?"

She swallowed and nodded. "If I'm going to use it, I should know how to do so properly and safely. Thank you."

***

Luc walked back from the target he'd set up ten yards away. He took up a position behind Eva and repeated the instructions. "Okay, release the safety catch, use two hands to steady your aim, sight and squeeze the trigger."

She tensed, shut her eyes and jerked the trigger. The explosion set off a cacophony of squawking in the trees and a flight of parrots took wing above their heads. Unprepared for the kick, she lurched backward into Luc's solid chest. His warm hands caught her elbows and he chuckled. "You won't hit anything if you close your eyes, Eva. And you need to squeeze the trigger, not jerk it. Like this."

He fitted his length against hers. Heat blazed down her spine as his body shaped hers, surrounding her. Every nerve sought closer contact with him until she was unsure where she ended and he began. The rasp of his stubbled chin against her cheek sent goose bumps down her right side and his warm breath fanned across her skin as he repeated his instructions in her ear. His hands closed over hers on the pistol.

Her head was cushioned against his shoulder and she nestled against the tanned column of his neck. A fraction of a turn of her head and her nose bumped into his chin. She closed her eyes and inhaled the most intoxicating scent she'd ever smelled. Old Spice aftershave mingled with clean, male sweat and images drawn from the pages of Josephine's diary. Heat rushed to that place between her thighs, moist and insistent and wanting, and her breath became choppy.

"You have to look at the target. Eva?"

She opened her eyes and tipped her head up. Mere inches from hers, his lips shaped her name. Such beautiful lips. The urge built within to trace their outline with her finger, her tongue, to taste them.

"Eva?"

She eased one hand from their joint hold on the gun and touched his cheek. Stubble scraped her fingers and a muscle jumped beneath her hand. He lowered the pistol and flicked on the safety catch before sliding it into its holster. In one smooth twist she turned into his arms and slipped hers around his neck.

He lowered his head and their mouths met in a kiss soft as spring rain. Her body trembled, heat zinged through her veins and pooled low in her belly. All their verbal sparring, their unexpected and heady attraction had been a prelude to this kiss. Prepared for fight or flight, her body chose close quarter action.

With a groan, Luc wrapped his arms around her, pulling her closer. His tongue swept between her parted lips and met hers.

He deepened the kiss and she met him with her own need and desire, sucking his lower lip and diving into his mouth to tangle with his tongue. Could she get closer? Pressed to his chest, her nipples rubbed against her bra and his muscles and responded by sending desperate messages to her core, which in turn pressed nearer to his thickening erection.

##

"Hey, boss, you up here, boss? Someone's shooting."

Luc reluctantly released Eva's lips and raised his head. The boys were headed this way and she was still very firmly pressed against him. Her reputation wouldn't survive the retelling if they were spotted wrapped around each other. And Sebastian was probably with them. What would he think if he saw his boss seducing his aunt?

He unholstered the pistol and placed it in her hand. "The boys are coming. Take the gun."

She blinked up at him. There was little he could do about her kiss-swollen lips or the pink mark where his stubble had scraped her soft skin but he could protect her reputation. He turned her to face the target once more and said roughly, "Eva, take aim and fire the damned gun. The boys are nearly here."

She ran her tongue across her lower lip and drew a deep breath. In one smooth movement, she raised the pistol, aimed, and fired as the boys emerged from the trees behind her.

"Woohoo! Way to go, Evie! You hit the target." Seb bounded up and applauded, followed by Acky and Moe. "When did you learn to shoot?"

"I've been giving your aunt a lesson. It seemed prudent after—last night."

"You mean the break in? Yeah, well, can I have a go, too?"

"If it's okay with your aunt?"

She cleared her throat and handed over the gun. "Don't let him take up too much of your time, Luc, and thank you—for the lesson." Pink blazoned in her cheeks and she turned quickly away.

"I'll pick you up at seven tomorrow night."

"What for? Oh, I don't think—"

"Seven. We're going to finish our *conversation*."

Chapter Eight

One kiss changed everything. And it changed nothing. Luc swung the axe and split the log with a satisfying *thwack*. So there were sparks between them. So Eva liked kissing him. So what? It didn't mean she liked him. It just meant she liked kissing him. *Thwack.*

Genevieve had enjoyed more than mere kisses. Not enough to consider marrying him but enough to risk her reputation. *Thwack.*

Seesawing between anger, lust, and frustration all afternoon, Luc directed his energy into the pile of uncut wood. What did he want from Eva? For her to succumb to his charm enough to sell the plantation? Or to fall into an affair with him? For all her skittishness, she had been as involved in that kiss as he was. He buried the axe head in the base block. Grabbing his canteen, he took a long swig of water and wiped his mouth on the back of his hand. Slinging the water bottle over his shoulder, he headed back to the house. His pretty neighbour stirred up a host of unwanted emotions and he was tired of taking cold showers.

Damn it. What had possessed him to invite her to dinner? And dancing? That would be the end of him. Holding Eva Abbott in his arms simply wasn't enough. So she'd softened toward him. It didn't mean she wanted more, even if he did.

Genevieve had only been slumming it with him. That betrayal rankled. Because he'd thought he was in love or because he'd been made to look like a callow fool? His eyes had been opened to the consequences of falling for an heiress and his heart wouldn't be engaged again.

But would an affair soften Eva? She cried poor. Until he saw that emerald necklace she'd worn in the photo, he'd believed her. He didn't need another reminder that, like Genevieve, and his mother, material riches were important to her.

He strode into his office and threw himself into a chair. Was an affair with Eva the answer? Concern for her nephew had led her to seek him out and her body had betrayed her attraction to him.

His gaze fell on the map of their two estates. Pencil markings cut through the boundary line joining the two plantations where the boys had begun cutting trees to open up a machinery track. His assumption and eagerness had almost cost him the chance to purchase her land. He wouldn't make that mistake again.

Coldblooded seduction of the heiress might win him her estate. This time, he wouldn't be deluded into falling for the woman. This time, he would stay in control.

The memory of Eva's eyes looking into his as he curtailed their kiss flashed through his memory. Hunger and desire had darkened their green but something more peeked at him. Was it trust? Or was she using their attraction to distract him?

He had to convince her to sell and their newly established truce provided the best opportunity so far. Ruthlessly, Luc suppressed the twinge of guilt that sliced through him.

***

Secluded in a corner of the veranda, candlelight and moonlight cast the planes of Luc's face into hard angles. If only she could see his eyes more clearly, know what he was thinking. Throughout the meal, they'd exchanged pleasantries. Soon there'd be no more small talk left and all that remained between them would be *that kiss*.

As the waiter removed their plates, Luc poured the last of the wine. "You're a real Annie Oakley with that pistol. The boys didn't stop talking about your uncanny ability all day and Seb's proud as punch."

"Honestly, I wasn't thinking about anything at the time. Can we not talk about it more—please?"

"Sure. There are other things we should talk about. That kiss for a start."

Her stomach clenched and she twirled her wine glass by the stem. *Not here, not now.* "No. Forget it happened."

He finished his wine and looked at her as he replaced his glass. "Ignoring it doesn't make it disappear. It happened."

"It shouldn't have. It won't happen again."

He laughed, and the sound was short and derisive. "Of one thing I'm certain, the sun has more chance of not rising tomorrow than that kiss being our last."

The intimacy of Luc's voice reminding her of that kiss warmed her traitorous body in places best not thought about in public. Josephine's descriptions had taken on deeper meaning and invaded her dreams with Luc in the starring role. Eva's cheeks heated and she glanced around the tables closest to them, hoping nobody had heard. "For heaven's sake, can we *please* not talk about it here?"

A breeze carrying the scent of the sea cooled her cheeks and she turned to look over the moonlit bay. A silver path led from the shore to the far horizon where an almost full moon rose from the water.

Luc turned her hand over and stroked his thumb across her wrist. "You can't tell me you feel nothing for me. Your pulse is racing."

She pulled her hand out of his and clenched it in her lap. "It doesn't matter what I feel. I have to think of Sebastian and what is best for him."

"You can't go through life ignoring your own needs."

"I have so far."

"It's not healthy. For instance, right now your body is swaying in time to the music." He skirted the table, pulled out her chair and offered his hand. "Dance with me?"

She flicked a quick look at the table beside them. The middle-aged woman caught her eye and smiled while her fingers tapped to the music. Refusing Luc wasn't an option because making a scene was out of the question. Reluctantly, she placed her hand in his, hoping one Foxtrot would satisfy him. Her luck was out.

Music segued into a waltz and he tightened his hold when she took a step toward their table. "Running away?"

Alive and sparkling with awareness of him, her body betrayed her with every move. Before she gave in to the simmering attraction, she needed distance. "I'd like to go home now. Please."

"As you wish."

Expecting a show of disappointment, she was perturbed by the quirk of his lips as he paid the bill, took her arm and led her to the car. Once he'd settled her into her seat he climbed in to his. Silence stretched for a mile or so before he broke it. "How's your new manager working out?"

Mundane conversation was much safer than dancing. She relaxed into the security of everyday detail. "He's competent. Since he arrived, the harvest has progressed efficiently and I've had no more visits from the pickers. I must thank Jack."

"Jack sent him?"

"Didn't you know? I assumed—never mind. Anyway, Stefan is a godsend."

"*Stefan?* What do you know about him? I haven't come across him before and Jack's not mentioned anyone of that name."

Innocuous as it was, Luc's inquiry made her question herself again. Her stomach churned about her rush to hire Stefan. Every decision had been so hard since Phillip's death, even her choice of manager. As if there had been any choice. She certainly couldn't have hired Luc—his terms were too high. She wished there was even one thing she could be certain about right now. Just one.

"What are you saying? Are you annoyed that I didn't accept your business proposition? If you're trying to make me feel guilty, it won't work."

He frowned and a muscle jumped in his cheek. "You had your reasons for refusing and I respect them. My offer still holds though. If you decide to sell, I would like first option to buy."

"*Mister Martineau*, if ever I should decide to sell, I'll be sure to let you know. But I fully intend to make Hawaii our home for the foreseeable future."

They coasted to a stop on the bluff and he switched off the engine.

"Why are we here?" And why hadn't her snippy remarks made him hightail for home? Starlight and moonlight played over the waves in a scene perfect for making out. Did he think to seduce her into agreeing to sell to him?

"Continuing our interrupted conversation. We called a truce, remember?"

The truce had led to *that kiss* she couldn't stop thinking about. She had to stop him before he kissed her again, before she gave in to the caress of his voice. Then Luc's fingers gently brushed her cheek and she leaned into his palm, aware her action was at odds with her attempts to maintain distance. Moonlight revealed the intensity of his gaze on her face, his focus on her mouth.

Slowly he leaned forward, warm breath fanning her skin and slipped his hand around to cradle her neck.

"We said all that needed saying."

"Then we're in agreement."

Her breath hitched. He was going to kiss her again. Butterflies flittered in her stomach. "If you think dinner and dancing and—and kissing will make me change my mind, you don't know me."

"Forget business for a few minutes, Eva. The only thing on my mind is kissing you. I've wanted to do this again all night."

His thumb stroked her cheek as he tipped her head back. Her body stilled as he lowered his mouth, his tongue tracing her top lip. She nibbled on his full bottom lip and he dipped into her mouth. Smoothing her hands up over his shoulders, she groaned with pent-up need and boldly met his tongue.

Tomorrow, she would berate her weakness but tonight, here and now, she needed to kiss him. Luc. Who wanted her land and would do whatever it took to get it.

She wrenched her mouth from his and sucked in a lungful of air.

Acrid smoke carried on the wind, stinging her eyes and making her cough. She grabbed his forearm. Wide-eyed, she scanned the trees on both sides. "I smell smoke."

He pointed behind them and started the engine. "It's coming from your side of the ridge."

"Oh, my God. Seb!"

Luc put the car into gear and drove quickly down the road with skill and fierce concentration. Minutes trickled by like sand in an hourglass until finally, they turned into her driveway. Crackling flames leapt into view as they tore around the last bend. He slowed the car and Eva jumped out before he came to a stop. Heat rolled out in fierce waves and she shielded her eyes against the glare. "Seb, where are you?"

Stay back." He sprinted past her to the burning building and a figure beating at the flames

Luc pulled him away as the walls collapsed inwards in a shower of sparks. Together, the two men staggered away from the shed, Luc half-dragging Seb.

She raced across to grab her nephew by the shoulders. "Seb. Oh, dear God. Are you okay?"

Luc lowered him to the ground and pushed his head to his knees. Seb coughed hard and dragged in lungfuls of smoky air while Eva hung on to his arm and patted his back. When he finally looked up, his face and clothes were covered in soot and sweat. "Sorry, Evie. Couldn't stop it."

She flung her arms around him. "You shouldn't have put yourself in danger like that."

"Here, lad, drink." Luc pushed a flask into Seb's hand and tipped it to his mouth. "How did the fire start?"

Seb took a long swig and wiped the back of his hand across his mouth, streaking soot into a bizarre slash of black around his white teeth. "I'm not sure. I was inside listening to the BBC broadcast of the cricket on the radio. Guess I dozed off during the break because the next thing I woke and smelled smoke. The shed was well and truly alight by the time I got out here."

Luc looked over at the dying blaze then fixed his gaze on Seb. "Did you see anyone or smell anything unusual?"

Unusual? He thought it might be arson? Seb flicked her a glance and gave Luc a sharp look. "Like petrol? No."

Fear shimmied down her spine. A petrol fire would have burned more fiercely, like the refinery fire during the London Blitz, which had spewed black smoke for days. "Where's Stefan? Have you seen him?"

"Not since I put the bike away when I got home. He asked if he could borrow it to go into town."

As if on cue, they heard the roar of Seb's motorbike climbing the driveway. Stefan pulled up beside Luc's car, dismounted and staggered slightly. As Stefan joined the little group huddled on the ground, he dropped to one knee beside Seb. "What happened? You okay, young boss?"

Slurred words confirmed her suspicion of alcohol but she held her peace for the time being.

Seb nodded and Luc helped him to his feet. "C'mon, Seb. You need a shower and bed. Eva, perhaps you could make him a hot drink while he cleans up."

She moved in and wrapped an arm around Seb's waist. He leaned heavily on her shoulder and she staggered under his weight. When had he beefed up?

He cleared his throat and stood straight. "I'm okay, Evie. I can walk."

"I know. I'm not sure I can right now though." She called

back over her shoulder. "I'll make coffee for you two as well. Come up to the house when you're ready."

"Thanks. We'll be there." Out of the corner of her eye, she saw him put out a hand to stop her manager and heard his request, even though he lowered his voice.

"Stefan, a word with you before you go."

Preoccupied with escorting Seb into the house, she heard no more. Once he was in the bathroom, she headed to the kitchen and put the coffee pot on.

Two bad events in three days was no coincidence.

She sank onto the nearest chair, clasped her hands together and concentrated on drawing in long breaths and slowly releasing them. Someone wanted to hurt her and Seb or at the very least, frighten them. But who was behind it and why?

Luc walked into the kitchen, a bottle of brandy in his hand. He held it out to her. "Thought you might need some in your coffee. Seb okay?"

She nodded. "He's having a shower. What did you say to Stefan?"

Luc sat and poured a shot of brandy into each cup before passing one to her. "I asked about the workers who've been here and we talked about security. He's checking the rest of the sheds now. You didn't tell me that Amoka threatened you. "

"I didn't want to read too much into it. I thought he was pushing because he didn't like taking orders from a woman. Anyway, Stefan turned up and dealt with him. Do you think Amoka was responsible or was this just an accident?"

Luc ran a hand through his hair. "It's possible but we won't know more until we can examine the remains of the shed. As for Amoka, I can't say I've heard anything bad about him or his crew before now, but they're fairly new to the area so we can't be sure." He paused and rubbed the back of his neck. "I want you and Seb to come home with me."

Eva looked up at him, shaking her head. "Surely you don't

think anyone is going to return tonight?"

"No. But I'll feel a whole lot better knowing you're with me."

So would she but there was no way she'd reveal that titbit to Luc. Where was her backbone? "What was the point of teaching me to shoot if you're not prepared to let us defend ourselves?"

"Eva—"

"I have a gun, I know which end to point and I *will* use it if I have to. And I will not let whoever is doing these things win by forcing us out of our home."

"Spending a night or two with me isn't letting them win. It's being sensible and safe."

How long had it been since she'd last felt like that?

Less than an hour ago in Luc's arms. Reliance on the handsome plantation owner was a weakness she couldn't afford, no matter how appealing the prospect. Not when she was still unsure of his motives. Not when she knew how he coveted her plantation. She shook her head. "What do you think people would say if we stayed overnight with you? Even if Seb is there, people will talk."

Luc's eyes narrowed and his Adam's apple bobbed up and down. "People talk all the time. Stefan agrees with me; it's safer if you and Seb aren't here. He'll stay and keep an eye on the place. Look, I don't want to alarm you but we suspect you're being targeted. The big question is why."

"I can't. Causing a scandal by moving into your home isn't the way to become a part of this community. Nor is running away when the going gets tough."

She looked up at his face reflected in the window, over her shoulder, and lit from behind like a dark angel. Their bodies assumed a single shape in the darkened glass. Behind her, the heat from him enveloped her and he rested his hands on her shoulders. "Then I'll stay here."

"How is that different from me staying at your home? No. Thanks for your concern but Stefan will keep us safe."

Chapter Nine

It had taken some convincing to get Eva to leave the repairs and clean up operation and accompany him to the Pineapple Festival and now they were here, she had disappeared with her picnic basket and a cheery 'back soon'. Luc leaned against the concession stand and glanced at the latest pageant of island beauties waiting for the winner to be announced.

"And Miss Pineapple Queen 1960 is—"

Jack strolled up and offered him a cold glass of juice. "Prettiest crop of Pineapple Princesses I've seen, don't you think?" They raised their drinks in silent salute and drank.

"I'm sure you'll find a willing partner from their ranks for the race." Luc turned and scanned the crowd for Eva's distinctive auburn hair. She'd hugged her picnic basket to her chest when he tried to carry it into the fair and refused to let him even peek at the contents.

"How can you blind bid if you know what's in the basket beforehand?" she'd said.

Could Eva cook? It seemed an odd achievement for an heiress. "How will I know if I want to eat what's inside if you don't show me?"

"Believe me, you'll want what's inside this package."

"Give me a clue then."

"Close your eyes."

He'd had to make do with guessing the contents from the delicious aromas wafting from her contribution to the annual fair. Not that it mattered. He intended to win her basket *and* her company for the picnic lunch.

"What is it with you?" Jack swept his glass in a broad gesture that encompassed the young women on stage eagerly crowding around to congratulate the winner. "Found yourself something more exotic, have you?"

"Huh?"

"Never thought I'd see the day you weren't interested in–"

"Piss off, Jack. Go console one of the princesses. I've got an auction to bid in." He ambled over to join the crowd gathering below the stage.

Jack strolled beside him. "Our heiress is a damn fine cook. You gonna bid for her basket?"

Were there hidden depths to Eva he hadn't suspected? *And how does Jack know things about her I don't?* "When did you taste her cooking?"

"You mean you haven't sampled her treats yet? You're slipping." Jack grinned and refused to answer.

Bidding got underway in the picnic hamper auction as they jostled for position. He tried to visualize Eva's basket as it sat on her lap in the Jeep and realized he'd paid more attention to the curve of her calf below her full skirt.

"What am I bid for this beautiful basket? Smells mighty tasty." The auctioneer peered in then closed the lid and placed the basket on the table. A huge bow in emerald green stirred in the breeze.

He was sure he's seen the bow brushing saucily against Eva's thigh when they arrived. He raised his hand. "Ten dollars."

"Twelve." Jack's spirited offer surprised and spurred him on.

"Fifteen."

"Sixteen. I know how good she cooks." Jack gazed beatifically at the basket and smacked his lips together.

"I brought her and I'm sure not letting you win this time, Jack. Twenty."

Amusement rippled through the crowd and speculative glances were thrown their way. It was the highest bid of the auction but he wasn't about to let Eva out of his sight.

Jack tutted in resignation. "You win, my friend. Enjoy lunch with our little heiress." He strolled a couple of steps before he turned back. "Besides, I just wanted to see how far you were prepared to go. Seems like the answer is *a long way*." He ambled away, whistling "Everybody's Somebody's Fool."

Luc shrugged and wandered over to pay for his prize at the table where Mitzy Stark guarded the cash box. She twitched the note from his fingers with a smile. "Is it pineapple pie you're hoping to lunch on or an English rose to chat up, Luc?"

"Maybe a bit of both, Mitzy." He winked, picked up his basket and turned to see Eva walking over to join him.

"So you're willing to bet on me cooking a decent lunch?"

"I was assured by an expert that your cooking is exceptional. Shall we?" Offering his arm, he led her to a shady spot a little apart from the throng. He put the basket against the base of the tree.

Eva handed him a small, tartan rug, which he spread, then she unpacked a deep-dish pineapple pie and assorted sandwiches and treats, a Thermos flask and cups. She smiled as she announced, "Luncheon is served."

Damn if Jack wasn't right. Eva's cooking was sensational. He patted his belly and sighed contentedly. "How does an English aristocrat learn to cook like this?"

"Necessity breeds creativity. Try cooking with only five ounces of butter per week."

"But you were barely a teenager when the war ended. Didn't you have a cook in Bellerose?"

"You think rationing ended with the end of the War? We struggled with rationed goods well into the fifties."

"I didn't know that. Sounds tough."

"It was the same for everyone. Would you like another helping?" She offered another slice.

He shook his head. "No. That was superb, thank you."

"I'll finish this piece—"

He touched her forearm. "You realise that, through winning your basket for lunch, you're also my partner in the charity race?"

"Pardon? You mean I have to run after that lunch?" She lowered the plate.

"Worse. I have to carry you."

Her eyes widened. "You're joking. Aren't you?"

"'Fraid not. Want to save that pie for afternoon tea?"

"Okay up there?" Luc held Eva's knees as she wriggled into position on his shoulders. Her full skirt fell down his back and left a tantalizing stretch of bare thigh in his line of view. He'd expected her to decline the challenge. Heiresses weren't known for risking either manicure or dignity in rowdy races but she'd surprised him. Again.

"As I'll ever be. What do I hold onto?"

"Whatever you like." He grinned. Eva's thighs tightened around his neck and suddenly, he wasn't laughing. Surrounded by her scent and heat, it hit him that her sweet core was pressed against the back of his neck. If he tried for a month of Sundays, he wouldn't have imagined being in this position with her. Other positions, maybe...

"Competitors ready..." The race marshal shuffled back from the line of men balancing young women on their shoulders.

Beside them, Jack crouched with the Pineapple Queen squealing on his shoulders.

"Go!"

"Go, Luc!"

Eva's command snapped him out of his dream state. He took off after Jack who was already leading the field.

Eva leaned forward and patted his head. "Faster!" He hadn't been a track star without learning how to push his body to the limits. They surged ahead of the rest of the field and he had Jack firmly fixed in his sights.

The Pineapple Queen screamed and covered Jack's eyes with both hands. Jack veered into the crowd, staggered to his knees, and both he and the Queen fell short of the tape.

Luc lunged for the line. Eva's weight shifted on his shoulders and threw them off-balance. Her victory shout became a shriek as she tumbled over his head. He landed on his knees beside the ice cream stand. Eva sat on her butt in a mud puddle.

She looked up and blinked. Laughter erupted around them and suddenly, she grinned. "We won."

He pushed to his feet and extended a hand to her. "Indeed we did. Great riding, partner!" He pulled her up. Two muddy hands landed on his chest.

"Next time, don't fall at the finish." She tapped his nose with her muddy finger.

"Sorry about that. And your outfit."

"What's a race without a little mud? I'll just go wash off the worst of it."

He watched her muddy backside all the way into the ladies' tent. Was it possible Eva wasn't the snobbish heiress he'd labelled her? She'd cooked up a dream, partnered him in a charity race and was laughing at a tumble in the mud. Preconceptions shattered and certainty fell by the wayside. Could he seduce her and still walk away?

Chapter Ten

Luc knocked a second time, waited and then stepped into Eva's hall. The squeal of heavy furniture being dragged across the library floor explained why no one had heard him knock.

"I think we've earned ourselves a break, Seb. What do you say to a cold drink?"

"Don't mind if I do, thanks. Hello, Eva." Luc walked into the room, looked around and whistled long and low. "Looks like one of those display rooms in a magazine."

Pink-cheeked, Eva scrambled to her feet and smoothed a hand over her hair. "Luc. I didn't hear you come in."

"I knocked but with all the banging coming from this room I guess you didn't hear me."
He looked from one to the other and chuckled. "Why don't you go pour those drinks, Seb? I need to speak to your aunt."

The teenager winked at him. "It might take me a while."

"No hurry."

He loped away.

Eva twisted a red scarf in her hands, and twitched at her tan shorts.

"You look fine."

"Are you a mind reader now?"

He grinned. Where she was concerned, it seemed he was.

Colour bloomed in her cheeks and she clutched her dusty scarf to her chest. "Was there a point to your visit other than to comment on my fashion sense?"

"I came over to check the boys' repairs to the shed and I ran into Stefan. He said the police report indicated the fire was started by an oil lamp. Difficult to say whether it was deliberate or not but they're calling it an accident."

She nodded and offered him a seat. "That's good for

insurance purposes. And I'd prefer to think it was accidental. The alternative is uncomfortable."

"Don't discount the other possibility, though. Two bad things seldom happen together."

"Now you're worrying me when I was starting to feel things had settled down."

"Just be careful to lock up."

"Thank you for sending Acky and Moe. They've done a great job helping Seb and Stefan with clearing the debris and erecting the new shed."

"Have you been sleeping okay?" God knew, he hadn't. The surge of protectiveness toward the woman and boy who had taken his dream from him, was uncomfortable and unwelcome. Softening his attitude to them wouldn't help him gain the land, despite the fun of the Pineapple Festival. But it was harder to remember his goal when she looked at him with her clear-eyed gaze. He folded his arms and leaned against the sofa.

She shrugged. "I kept the gun near my pillow. I tried putting it underneath but I felt like the princess with the pea."

He raised an eyebrow. "Should I know what you mean?"

"It's an English fairy story. Anyway, I was so aware of the bulk of it lying beneath my pillow I still couldn't sleep. Now I keep it on the night stand."

"No chance of you sleepwalking?"

"Very droll. Perhaps you should leave while you can still walk."

"Threatening me, Eva? Play nice or you won't come to dinner at my home on Friday."

"What a gallant invitation. How could a girl resist, but I will try."

Luc's smile disappeared. Gallant would never apply to his behaviour around her. They struck sparks as they skirted around the elephant in the room but in spite of the fact she had his plantation, he enjoyed the spice of their encounters.

"Please come. My father's returning to Hawaii and he's bringing his new fiancée with him. The dinner's a welcome home." A bitter note crept into his voice.

Eva reached out and touched his arm. "I thought you got on well with your father."

His jaw muscles clenched. "Yeah, we do, but his taste in women is terrible. Witness my mother."

"You're prejudging his fiancée, the poor woman, and that's not fair. Just because your mother didn't live up to your expectations—"

That emotional baggage where his mother was concerned was well known but had it dawned on Eva why Genevieve Benson had rejected his proposal of marriage? The social stigma of his mother's adultery and divorce was as strong as ever in the islands.

"That's a laugh. My mother was always the good time girl, even during the war. The sniff of a party and she'd be pulling on her silk stockings."

"All women aren't the same. Not everyone is just out for a good time. At least give your father's fiancée a chance before you condemn her, sight unseen." Her words niggled at him, at his willingness to believe the worst of Eva.

He pressed his lips together and nodded. "I'll try. Will you come? As a friend."

"It sounds as though it should be a family reunion. I'd hate to intrude."

He took her hand between his and brushed her knuckles with his thumb. "I want you there because I know you won't let me say something I might regret. You can bring your gun if you like."

A ghost of a smile touched her lips but didn't quite reach her eyes. "I might be too tempted if you misbehave. Better leave it under my pillow."

"Spoilsport. Tell me about this magazine thing." Playful Luc emerged and he grinned as the conversation moved to safer topics.

"They're coming to interview me tomorrow, a journalist and a photographer."

***

Eva gestured the two men from the magazine to the sofa and poured cold drinks for them. The young photographer, Ben, fiddled with his camera. He looked barely more than Seb's age and her heart sank a little. It was probably foolish and a little naïve but she'd hoped the magazine might be one of the bigger ones who paid for interviews. Any amount to pay off the mortgage would be welcome.

Mr Kowalski, the journalist, gave her a wide, white-toothed grin and pulled out a notebook and pen. "Thanks for talking with us, Miss Abbott. Nice spread you've got here."

She offered the tray of drinks and each man took a glass. "Frankly, I was surprised when your editor rang asking for the interview. I still don't understand why my family history is of interest to your magazine."

"Since Hawaiian statehood, we're running a feature series on new beginnings and you, Miss Abbott, are a fascinating link between the Old World and our fiftieth state of the Union."

"Your editor said you had some questions about my family connections in New Orleans, is that right? How does my family history fit with new beginnings?"

"Well now, you mentioned to the photographer back in New Orleans that you had a pirate ancestor. He passed that on to our editor, along with the fact that you were en route to Hawaii to take over a pineapple plantation. That's a mighty big undertaking for a lone woman."

"I see. So is it the romantic pirate past or the modern woman taking on a man's role that your editor wants to use?"

Mr Kowalski opened his mouth and then closed it without a word. He and Ben turned to each other and a look passed between them that she couldn't interpret. Caution seemed the wisest course until she knew more.

"Let's start at the beginning with that newspaper photo. Who was the woman in the portrait?" Kowalski looked at her, pencil poised over his notebook.

Unable to pinpoint what it was about the men that made her uneasy, Eva took a moment to answer. Maybe she was seeing shadows everywhere because of the past couple of weeks.

"My ancestress, Josephine Dubois, married a French merchant, Francois, in New Orleans in the late eighteenth century."

"And he gave her that necklace? Do you still have it?"

"I thought this meeting was to discuss my family history."

Kowalski shrugged, apparently unconcerned by her tone. "I'm getting to that. What stones are in the necklace, emeralds and diamonds?"

"Unfortunately, I've never seen the real piece."

He pulled out a newspaper clipping, a copy of the photo she had framed on the mantel. "So, your ancestress, Josephine, had this necklace and passed it on to her niece who married a pirate. Is that right?"

"I assume it was passed on, although I believe her nephew-in-law was not so much a pirate as an abolitionist."

"What do you suppose the niece and her pirate husband did with the necklace?"

"I have no idea what happened to the piece after Josephine had her portrait painted but Madeleine and Sebastien Leclerc eventually settled here in the Hawaiian Islands. He wasn't following the pirate trade then, Mr Kowalski. Just a land owner with a sizable plantation."

"And is this the property they owned? Is that why you bought this place?" Ben chimed in for the first time, reminding her yet again of Seb's boyish enthusiasm. "Do you think they buried the necklace here? Are you going to dig for—"

"Enough, Ben. You're out of line." Kowalski's gruff reprimand caused a dull red to creep up Ben's cheeks.

Eva smiled at the photographer, more willing to deal with

him than his older partner. "It's okay. My nephew was speculating on the same thing, only he doesn't think there'd be any digging involved."

"Ben, would you take a couple of shots of Miss Abbott, then you can go and talk to her nephew."

"Cool." Ben jumped to his feet, camera at the ready. "Miss Abbott, would you mind turning a little to your right please?"

"Happy to oblige, Ben. Like this?"

He clicked off a couple of shots and looked at his boss. "Do you want me to take some of the pineapple fields?"

"Sure. Off you go."

Ben hurried away, camera swinging against his chest and Kowalski sat back. "So, Miss Abbott, what made you choose Hawaii and pineapple farming for your new life?"

***

Eva waved and watched Seb drive off with his new friend, Ben, until the taillights were out of sight. Even without moving far, a trickle of sweat slid down her back. How she wished she could wear her hair up. She slipped an arm under the mass of hair and lifted it, raising her face to a cooling breeze. With a sigh, she let her hair fall and turned to knock on Luc's door.

He was standing in the doorway watching her, his gaze intent. Her breath caught in her throat. Had he seen her scars? She waited for the look of revulsion that Timothy had worn; the look that had said he was worth more than a wife who was damaged goods. Even with a fortune she'd barely been acceptable to him. Without one, who would look at her?

Luc strolled across and raised her hand to his lips. "Good evening, Eva. You look beautiful."

Her knees turned to water and her hand tightened in his. He hadn't seen. He didn't know. Relief coursed through her body and she swallowed the knot of fear in her throat. When she smiled, perhaps a little more brightly than usual, his gaze flicked to her mouth. Heat bloomed in her secret places like a tropical flower.

She ran her tongue across her top lip and his gaze zeroed in on her mouth.

"Ah, Eva. You really are well named."

If she was Eve in the Garden, was Luc Adam, or the serpent? For tonight, it didn't matter. She knew what he wanted, and forewarned was forearmed.

The overhead light highlighted a blue-black sheen in his hair and picked up the satin of his single-breasted jacket. The shawl collar and lack of vest was so unlike the boxy double-breasted jacket and sharp lapels still being worn back in England. Instead, the tailored look and soft evening shirt emphasised his athletic physique. She pressed her thighs together. "You scrub up pretty well yourself." Was that breathy voice really hers?

"It's amazing what a suit can do for a man." He leaned toward her, his mouth mere inches from hers, their breath mingling. She tipped her head back in welcome of what must surely follow.

"Luc?" A voice called from within the house and broke the spell.

He stepped back and offered his arm. "That's my father."

A ridiculous sense of disappointment rushed through her and Eva quashed the need to press into his chest. Smudged lipstick and mussed-up hair were not the best look when meeting other guests. But where Luc was concerned, it seemed common sense deserted her, despite her resolve to keep her distance until she knew where she stood with him.

"Come in and meet dad. He's anxious to meet you."

They entered the reception room where two people sat close together on the sofa. Both rose as he drew her forward. "Eva, this is my father, Henri, and his fiancée, Jayne Dwyer."

Henri took her hand, kissed it and bowed. "*Enchanté*, Eva. It's about time this rogue of mine found a good woman and—"

"*Suffis, papa. Ne parle plus de ça.*"

Her French was excellent and she understood the sharp

request but what did Luc not want his father saying? Henri stiffened. Father and son locked gazes and an unspoken message passed between them. A muscle jerked in Henri's jaw before he turned back to her and smiled gently. "I am pleased to meet you, *ma belle*. Welcome to paradise."

He released her hand and slipped his arm around his fiancée's waist. "And this other beautiful woman has, for her sins, agreed to be my wife."

Jayne's brown hair was pinned into a graceful chignon and her blue eyes sparkled in a face that became pretty when she smiled up at Henri. A solitaire engagement ring sparkled on her finger as Jayne extended both hands to Eva. "It is lovely to meet you. How lucky you are to live in such a beautiful place. Luc was telling us you sold everything to move here with your nephew."

"We couldn't afford to stay in Bellerose after the government death taxes."

"Oh, my dear, what a difficult decision to have to make, but a very brave one."

She warmed immediately to the older woman's charm and it was easy to see Jayne cared deeply for Luc's father.

Jayne steered the conversation around to more general topics and soon statehood and the tourism prospects were being discussed with much enthusiasm as the first course was served.

Luc turned to his father. "Tourist numbers have already risen well beyond what I thought they would."

Henri nodded. "Seems you were right about the potential."

"These men and their work." Jayne leaned closer to Eva. "Tell me more about Bellerose. Did you have beautiful gardens there?"

By the time dessert was cleared, Eva felt as though she had known Jayne all her life. Calm, competent, and comfortable to be around, Henri had found a wonderful woman. Surely Luc would be satisfied with his new stepmother.

Jayne looked around with a smile. "Shall we take coffee on

the veranda? I do declare there's more of a breeze out there now."

Luc stood and pulled her chair out while Henri did the same for Jayne and the party moved to the veranda. Eva wandered over to the edge and leaned on the teak railing. A sea breeze cooled her cheeks and she slipped a hand under her hair and lifted it off her neck.

Jayne reached over and smoothed an errant curl off her shoulder. "Such a beautiful colour, like Rita Hayworth. But why don't you put your hair up in this hot weather? Lovely as it is—"

Luc's lazy drawl cut into their conversation. He leaned against a post and eyed her closely. "Why confine such glory with pins and whatever else you women use? Besides, I like Eva's hair lush and a little wild."

Eva forced a smile and Jayne returned to the coffee table.

How dare he imply he'd seen her in such a state? She finished her coffee and gripped her cup to stop from reaching up her hand to smooth her hair.

Luc gently removed it from her grip. "Well, delightful as this evening has been, I think it's time I took Eva home."

"Please don't bother. I can phone Seb."

"I did promise him I'd take you home."

"When?"

"When he told me he was borrowing your car tonight and asked if I could see you home."

Jayne stepped forward and took hold of her hands. "It was lovely to meet you. We look forward to seeing much more of you while we're here. Good night, dear." Jayne kissed her cheek and gave her a kindly smile, followed by Henri. In true Gallic fashion, he kissed both cheeks and, with a cheerful good night, followed Jayne into the house.

***

Luc handed over her gloves and bag and offered his arm for the walk to the car. He opened the door and assisted her into her seat. Floral perfume and anger rolled off her skin. He tucked her full skirt in before shutting the door. "Do you want to tell me now, Eva?"

"Tell you what? Tell you off for making personal remarks that imply something more about our relationship?"

He grinned, climbed into his seat and started the engine. Eva's presence had made an evening with his father and new stepmother pleasant, and his newfound mellowness sparked a sense of mischief. "What more would you like there to be?"

"Nothing. There is nothing between us." She gritted her teeth and twisted her gloves into a tight roll.

"Who are you trying to convince? Don't start lying to yourself. You're honest about everything else. Why not about us?"

"There's a you, and there's a me. There is no *us*, Luc." She twisted her hands together in her lap, wrinkling her gloves in the process and gazed at the passing landscape.

She was wrong. No matter his pursuit of her had begun with the sole intention of softening her up to gain her land. Now, he wanted that affair with her. Maybe once he'd bedded her he could get back to planning the expansion of his program.

In her current state of mind, it seemed she didn't notice where he was driving to, until he pulled up on the same bluff he'd stopped at before. The moon rode high in the sky but in the south, dark clouds filled the horizon. Reflecting her mood? He liked her passionate side when she dared let her social façade slip. Could he coax it out tonight?

"What are we doing here? I want to go home."

"Not yet. Not until you give me an honest answer, Eva." He moved to her side of the car and opened the door.

She folded her arms and refused to budge.

"You're misguided if you think ignoring me will make me give up." He held his hand out and waited. "We can do this the easy way or the hard way."

"Hard? You wouldn't dare." She turned away from him.

"Then you don't know me very well. I can and I will." He

waited, hand at the ready to assist her. "On second thought, don't move. The hard way is much more fun."

He scooped her out of her seat and backed her against the side of the car, trapping her by the simple expedient of placing his hands on the car either side of her waist.

Her body was close to his and he leaned in until only clothing separated their heat. Green eyes like twin pools of desire blazed at him and he slid his fingers into her hair and tipped her face to his.

"We're two consenting adults, Eva. Why shouldn't we enjoy each other?"

Despite her obvious resolve to avoid entanglements with him, her body had other ideas. Under the light of a full Hawaiian moon, her lips parted and she closed the last inch separating their mouths.

Fierce elation rose within him as the ridge of his erection pressed against her stomach, thick and clear in invitation. He whispered along her collarbone and she tipped her head to give him better access to the column of her neck. At her earlobe, he stopped and gently bit. She nipped his neck and a pleasurable yet aching need shot through him. He cupped her breast and dropped heated kisses along the creamy swell of soft skin.

She tugged his head back to her lips while his other hand shaped her hip.

"I want you." He kissed the delicate skin beside her mouth, trailed kisses over her temple as his arousal pressed into her stomach, evidence of his desire. "Let's go back to your place and take this to its natural conclusion. I want to make love to you and I want to do it in a bed where I can admire your beautiful body. I want to kiss every inch of your skin."

She gasped and pushed him away.

"What's wrong?"

"This. You—me. I can't, Luc. Please, let me go."

Confused, he blocked her retreat and took hold of her wrist

and pulled her close. "Why?"

"It won't work. I'll make a bigger fool of myself than I already have."

Did she mean the heiress making out with the plantation boss? He was the fool and the laugh was on him. It was Genevieve all over again. He dropped her hand as though it scalded him.

She stepped around him. Without looking back, she grabbed her bag and gloves and walked away down the track.

He'd allowed this crazy attraction to her to threaten the walls he'd built to hide his bruised heart. There would be no more rejections. From now on, his business and his program would take priority. And pretty Eva Abbott had best beware because he was going to win her plantation, whatever it took.

Chapter Eleven

Sunrise tinged the sky as Luc reversed out of the garage. Movement on the veranda caught his attention as his father waved and hurried down the stairs. "Luc. Where are you heading?"

"The south fields. The pineapples are almost ready for picking."

"Mind if I ride with you?" His father strode up to the Jeep and climbed in.

Company was the last thing Luc wanted after last night's debacle with Eva but how could he refuse? "You're up early. Thought you'd sleep in for the first day or two after the flights."

"Planter's time. Hard to break the habit. How is the Smooth Cayenne variety doing? Did you stay with them?"

"Most of the fields are planted with Smooth Cayennes, like you selected. They seem to be the most productive but I'm trying a different variety in the south field. A crossbreeding program using the Ruby Queen."

"Imported varieties need a different approach. They can take a while to acclimatize and need a little more attention until they put down solid roots. But it's worth persevering for the end result."

"Why do I get the feeling you're not talking about pineapples any more?" A knot of tension hardened in his shoulders. Eva was off limits as far as conversation with his father—or anyone else for that matter—went.

Eva. Why had she pulled back from him last night? She had been as ready as him to make love in the car. Mention of going to her home and making love seemed to have been the turning point.

Shit! Seb. How could he have forgotten? Because his brains had been down in his trousers poking at Eva.

His father eyed him speculatively. "Your English rose could do well here. She's not as delicate as she looks, but you could hurt her if you're not careful. Jayne was saying—"

"None of your damned business or your fiancée's."

"Eva's the kind of woman you make a life with, Luc. She's reserved but she's worth the extra time and effort."

So even his father was bewitched by Eva. Hadn't his wife's betrayal soured him?

"Eva is none of your business and nor is my love life. Just drop it, will you?" His father was mad if he believed his son would contemplate getting seriously involved with another woman. Had he forgotten how Genevieve had led him on, then told him he was good enough to fuck but not to marry?

"You've been carrying a thorn in your side about women since your mother ran out on us. It can eat away inside until there's nothing left but a hollow shell of a man. Believe me, I know. If it hadn't been for Jayne—"

"And now you're engaged to Jayne. Do you think she'll be any different from your first wife?"

His father's hands clenched on his thighs but he maintained an even tone of voice. "She's completely different with a whole different attitude to life. And love."

"Don't tell me you believe in that nonsense. After all my mother put you through, I can't believe you are really going to do that whole till death do us part thing again."

"Listen to yourself. I look at you and it's like seeing myself after your mother left. Bitter and twisted and destined to be alone for the rest of your life. Do you really want that?"

He clenched the wheel and swerved harder than necessary to avoid a pothole. Bitter and twisted? Was that really how his father saw him? Was that how Eva viewed him? "Why give any woman power over me? Neither mother nor Genevieve actually inspired me to trust." Even a green-eyed, red-haired goddess who made him forget everything when she was in his arms.

"It's unfortunate the two women who should have been your gold standard turned out to be base metals but unless you take a chance, you're going to be a lonely man for a very long time."

"I took a chance, remember? Fat lot of good it did me."

"Genevieve was greedy but at least she was upfront about what she wanted from marriage, unlike your mother. Don't measure other women against her."

"And you're willing to risk everything again on Jayne?"

"I'd give up everything to be with her. She saved me from myself."

"A touching story, Dad, but I prefer to depend on myself and no one else."

His father put a hand on his shoulder and squeezed. "I just hope you come to your senses before you lose your chance with Eva."

Luc pulled up at the edge of the south field and parked under a tree. "I'll be back soon." He strode off down the nearest row, muttering under his breath. His father was a fool who was going to get hurt again and there wasn't a damned thing he could do to stop it.

He rubbed a hand over his face and wiped grit from his eyes. Restless and frustrated by Eva's sudden departure, he had tossed and turned for long hours, finally giving up on sleep. The attraction sizzling between them was reciprocated—her ardent kisses assured him of that—and yet she'd pushed him away as soon as he'd mentioned going to bed. What did she want from him? A wedding ring?

It would be a cold day in hell before he gave Eva the sort of power Jayne had over his father.

***

Eva fumed as she marched along the rows of pineapples. Unable to find Stefan or Seb, her mood darkened further. Last

92

night's almost disastrous conclusion reminded her that Luc was her enemy. His wild kisses, this dark passion he aroused in her, she couldn't afford to succumb to it. Not for the first time, she wondered if his plan was to seduce her to gain her plantation. Even his best friend, Jack, had said Luc would do anything to get what he wanted.

She stomped on, checking up and down the slope for her manager. Stefan needed to know that, from now on, Luc was *persona non gratis* around here and Seb—Seb would just have to accept her word for once. Keeping her handsome neighbour at arm's length was the only means she could think of to maintain her equilibrium.

Her stomach clenched at the thought of that conversation. Seb admired Luc, too much for his own good, but the friendship wasn't real. Somehow she had to make him see that Luc was using him to get their property. Sweat trickled down her back and she realized she'd left her hat in the Jeep. Shade beckoned at the end of the row and she stepped into cooler air with a small sigh of relief.

Bright sunlight washed out the midday colour of the fruit. She brushed the back of her hand across her forehead and shaded her eyes, searching for the dark shirt of her overseer amid the green of the pineapples.

The sound of voices echoed up from the bottom of the hill. Stefan moved into view but before she could call and wave to him, a second figure joined him, gesturing emphatically.

Kowalski? What was he doing here, and what did he have to talk about with her manager? Unless he was digging for dirt for that article. She glided silently into the shade behind the tree trunk.

The two men continued up the track, heading toward her, and she scouted for a way to retreat before they discovered her. The ludicrous nature of the situation hit when she reminded herself this was her plantation. She stepped out from the tree cover. "Good morning, gentlemen."

The two men and their conversation came to an abrupt halt.

Stefan's eyes narrowed and he stood stolidly in the middle of the path. Kowalski advanced a couple more steps, removed his hat and inclined his head. "Miss Abbott. Hello again. I was just getting some background information on how a plantation runs. It sounds like a great deal of work and little things going wrong can cause big problems."

"Like what?"

"Like the attitudes of workers to a female owner. But this is just the sort of topic our readers will devour. New state, new beginning, new way forward. Do you like that, Miss Abbott? I think it suits you." His smile invited her confidence but she was disinclined to humour him.

"There's no reason why a woman can't own and operate a plantation. It doesn't matter whether one is male or female, having the right staff is the key and I'm very fortunate to have Mr Luchenko. Speaking of whom, I need a word with you, Stefan."

"Sure, boss."

Kowalski inclined his head again and replaced his hat. "I'll leave you for now, Miss Abbott. Would you mind if I have a bit of a wander around and if Ben takes more photos while we're here?"

"By all means. Good day, Mr Kowalski."

He flashed his wide grin and, hands in pockets, wandered back down the track, whistling.

Eva waited until he was out of earshot before meeting Stefan's shadowed eyes. "Was that really all he wanted, Stefan?"

"Sure. He want to know how one lone woman handle men workers. I tell him you fair boss and you got me"—he stabbed at his chest with his thumb—"Stefan Luchenko, to help."

She nodded and checked on Kowalski's progress down the hill. "I'm grateful you're here."

"What for you look for me?"

"Mr Martineau is no longer welcome on this plantation and Seb is not to go down there anymore. It makes more sense for him to learn on his own property than elsewhere. I wondered if you would be willing to teach him what you know?"

Stefan looked over the field and up at the house without speaking, and she worried she'd overstepped some invisible mark in the employer-employee relationship. "Of course, if you don't feel you can then—"

"I do it for you. But he must stand on own two feet. I not baby him."

"Thank you. If I see him, I'll send him to find you." At least that was one thing sorted. But she still had to tell Sebastian. Her appetite disappeared as she trudged back to the Jeep.

***

Red lights danced behind Eva's eyelids and she cracked one eye open. Morning sun filtered through the gap between the curtains, warm and toasty on her feet. Eva sat up suddenly and clamped a hand to her forehead. She'd fallen asleep fully dressed and slept through the night, missing the chance of talking to Seb, because he'd spent the evening with Ben.

With a grimace, she pulled her rumpled clothes off and headed for the shower, hoping Seb hadn't already left for Luc's place. Dread of that conversation was partly responsible for the headache that had plagued her yesterday.

Seb knocked on the door and called, his voice distant through the splashing water. "Evie? I'm going to Luc's. See you tonight."

"Seb? Wait, I'm coming." She turned off the shower, grabbed her bathrobe from the hook and shoved her arms into the sleeves. Rapidly tying the belt, she pulled the door open.

"I gotta go, Evie. I'll be in trouble if I'm late. One of Luc's rules. Can't it wait till tonight?"

"You won't be going back to Luc's. Stefan is going to teach you all you need here on your own plantation." Words tumbled from her mouth. If he left now, she might not find the courage to tell him later.

Seb looked at her and frowned, his tone snarky. "Haven't

we been through this all before?"

She'd known this would be a hard conversation but why did it have to be so difficult? The image of Luc's piercing gaze before she'd marched away from him haunted her. She swallowed the lump in her throat and met his gaze. "He's our neighbour. There's no reason to fight with him. Why on earth would you think I'd have a fight with him?"

"I think you like Luc. He sure likes you but you keep pushing him away and I'm caught in the middle."

Was she taking out her distrust of Luc on Seb? "This is about what's fair and reasonable. I can't pay Luc for your training and I can't agree to give him a share of the plantation in exchange for his help. It will be your inheritance one day."

"Luc wouldn't ask for anything like that. He'd do it for free. He's cool."

If he only knew what Luc wanted but she wouldn't destroy his illusions about his boss. Not when Luc had helped them. "While Stefan is here and we're paying his wage, it makes sense for you to learn from him, on your own plantation."

"Have you told Luc yet? Can I at least ride over and tell the guys?"

She noted the American slang filtering into his speech. Seb was transitioning to island life faster and more easily than she was, courtesy of Moe and Acky. Not that she hadn't expected it to happen, just not so quickly. "That will be fine, but you need to be back here to work with Stefan on the eastern field in an hour. The boys will be working at Luc's too, remember."

Muttering under his breath, he stalked from the house. Seconds later, the bike roared away.

Bringing up a teenage boy on her own was challenging in ways she'd not expected. Eva sighed as feelings of inadequacy threatened to swamp her. Swallowing down her grief and self-pity, she dressed in work clothes before she settled in her office to phone the outlet about a returned delivery. How could pineapples get damaged anyway? The fruit was so heavy and solid. Was it possible someone had sabotaged the process? Maybe Luc could tell her what—

No more running to him with her problems. She'd preached self-sufficiency to her nephew and she would live by her words.

She lifted the receiver and put through her call. Two soft clicks sounded while she waited to talk pineapples with the manager. Was someone else on the party line? "Hello? Anyone there?" Receiving no response, she tapped the earpiece against her palm, heard nothing more, and tucked the phone between her shoulder and ear.

The solicitor's letter lay on the top of her small pile of mail. Family lawyers for several generations, Mr Johnson, of Bates and Johnson, was about the only male she did trust right now. She slit the envelope open and took out the letter. She smoothed the letter flat with her palm and scanned the contents. Pressing her lips together, Eva swallowed. Her eyes pricked as she blinked back tears.

Bellerose was no longer theirs.

In addition, it seemed she and Seb could not afford to live if the plantation wasn't a commercial success. She swiped at the moisture on her cheeks.

Could they live off the land? Maybe she could write a cookbook in which pineapple featured as the main ingredient— breakfast, lunch and dinner dishes starring the Islands' very own sunshine fruit. If only she had Josephine's emerald necklace. *Then I'd be the one selling off precious stones to survive.*

She tossed the solicitor's letter on the desk and picked up a pencil, reworking sums on the back of the empty envelope until a gruff voice demanded to know what she wanted.

By the time she replaced the receiver, she had arranged to meet the outlet owner and had learned enough to know what to discuss with Stefan about packing the fruit better.

Doubt about his capability crept in. Surely an experienced

manager would have known not to overfill the bins for transport? It seemed such a simple concept but she would give him a chance to explain.

Ideas to generate more money jostled in her brain, among them a plan to turn their plantation into a tourist attraction. The outlet owner had mentioned a Tourism Board contract that she was determined to try for. Applications closed in a couple of days and she would have to work fast but the opportunity was too good to miss. Such a contract would assure a steady income and increase their chances of making a go of the place. They needed a new name, something catchy and fresh to appeal to tourists and the Board as well. Sun Pines? Sunshine Pines?

High-pitched bursts of metal on stone led her to the shed where Stefan was sharpening knives on a whetstone wheel. Sparks flew, dropping harmlessly on the stone floor. She eyed the blades with distaste and moved further back. He switched off the wheel and tossed the blade he'd sharpened, deftly catching it. He handled the blade as though it was an extension of his left arm. Finally, his dark gaze locked on hers. Cold seeped into her bones. She swallowed the lump of fear in her throat. "It seems we have a problem with the packing of the fruit going to the outlet store. Almost a quarter of it was rejected because the boxes were overfilled. We can't afford to have that happen again."

He sat back on his stool and tapped the tip of the knife against his chin, his gaze unblinking.

She edged a step closer to the door and tucked her hair behind her ear. "You won't let that happen again, will you?"

Abruptly, he surged to his feet and the stool fell with a clatter. Heart hammering in her chest, she fixated on the knife in his big hands. No wonder Amoka had backed off. Why hadn't she checked him out, even confirmed his background with Jack Lyons? Yet, Luc had met him, and said nothing.

Slowly, Stefan sheathed the knife and folded his arms across his chest. "I try to save you money. Not so many boxes, cost less for transport. Back home in Russia, this is what we did with vegetables. Will not do it again."

Her bones melted as relief coursed through her body. "That was good of you to consider costs, but our reputation needs to be built on a quality product. We can't take shortcuts in future." She pasted on a smile and slipped out the door.

One down, two to go. Next stop was the Tourism Board.

Eva dressed in her best suit, smoothed her hair into a sleek chignon style, and carefully tucked a scarf around her neck. Satisfied that she looked the part of a businesswoman with a sound proposal, she drove to the Tourism Office in town.

A friendly receptionist directed her to a waiting area filled with bright-green, potted palms. "Mister Willis won't be long, ma'am. He's just with another client. Can I get you a coffee or water?"

Eva smiled and shook her head. "Thank you, no." She took a seat beside a corridor that led to offices behind her and waited. During the drive into town, she'd formulated a general proposal in her head but if the manager wanted to know financial position details, her chances were sunk.

A door opened behind her and a voice carried down the corridor. "The program you're running puts your place in a really good light. The Board will love it, even without the other property. Your chances of scoring the contract are very good."

Eva sat very still and held her breath. Were the men referring to the tourist contract? Had someone beaten her to it before she even applied?

"Thanks for that, Dan. 'Preciate the vote of confidence. My boys are shaping up fine."

Luc.

She clutched her handbag and forced her tight facial muscles to shape a pleasant social smile. Determined not to let him win this time, she stood to face the two men just as they rounded the corner.

Luc stopped mid-sentence and his eyes raked her from top to toe. "Miss Abbott. What an unexpected pleasure to see you here."

"Isn't it? Please don't let me hold you up, Mr Martineau. I know how busy you are." She turned and held out her hand to the older man and broadened her smile. "How do you do, Mr Willis? I'm so glad you could make time to see me today."

Luc sat on the edge of the sofa in the reception area and flicked over another page in the newspaper without a clue as to what he'd read. Why was Eva meeting with Willis? Was it possible she was chasing the tourism contract, too? And what was going on with Seb? According to Moe, Seb had roared up to the shed on his bike with a thunderous expression on his face, given some garbled account of having to work with Stefan from now on, and roared away again before Luc could speak to him. Poor kid didn't know what the hell was going on and neither did he.

He ground his teeth and imagined taking Eva's sweet little neck between his hands and... and what? As soon as he had her that close, he'd forget why he was angry with her and kiss her senseless. Every time he thought of her, it involved peeling her clothes off and losing himself in her silken body, tasting her from her delectable lips all the way to the sweet juncture between her thighs. Conquering the heiress and winning her into his bed was becoming an obsession.

Luc groaned softly and edged further back in the seat to ease his burgeoning erection.

He wasn't a quitter. He never had been. If there was the slightest hope of winning the contract, he'd take it. Barry Willis's throwaway comment had given him an idea. His best chance now rested on collaborating with Eva.

The receptionist glanced over at him. He nodded with a tight smile, and raised the paper between them, thankful he hadn't picked up a magazine instead.

Eva emerged from her meeting with Willis, a frown wrinkling her forehead and so absorbed in her thoughts she walked straight past him. Luc lowered the newspaper, tossed it aside as he stood, and walked over to take her arm. "I think it's time you and I had a really good talk, Miss Abbott."

"But I don't—"

"Come on, I'm buying you coffee." Maybe if he talked to her in a public place, where touching her was out of the question, they could reach a compromise about the land and move on to more pleasant pastimes. Damn pleasant. He wanted to sink into her and never surface.

They walked into the King Kamehameha Hotel lounge and Luc ordered a pot of coffee, before he led Eva to a table by the window.

"What do you want?"

"Can't neighbours have a friendly chat?"

He glanced around to see if anyone was watching them. An older couple he recognized from the Planters' Club turned and stared. The woman raised her eyebrows, picked up her cup, and looked away. Nobody could know about this proposition until he had it in the bag. He lowered his voice and leaned closer. "This business with Seb has got to be sorted out now."

Eva sat back into her chair and lifted her chin. "It's sorted. He's going to learn from Stefan, on the plantation that will be his own. It's what I should have done in the first place."

"But you didn't. You asked for my help."

She had the good grace to look abashed. "I'm very sorry for the inconvenience I've caused you. Thank you for what you did for Seb. I really appreciate it but he's no longer any of your business."

"You gave him a taste of what it's like to belong within a group of young men, to begin the healing process after his father's death, and then ripped him away from his friends. Is that fair? It's not so much an inconvenience to me but have you been fair to the boy?" He paused to watch her reaction.

Eva twisted the strap of her handbag on her lap and would not meet his gaze. Luc waited but there was no reply forthcoming. For the boy's sake, and for the contract, he would change her mind. He pressed on. "Did you ask him what he wanted? I know you care deeply for him and want what's best but right now, he's an angry young man. He doesn't know what's going on and frankly, neither do I."

"As his guardian, I have to make decisions about what's in his best interests. I happen to think learning from Stefan on my estate is in his best interest."

"Bullshit."

Her eyes widened. She opened her mouth and drew an audible breath then closed it without speaking.

"You're letting what's between you and me affect your thinking. Seb's happy and committed to learning with me. You know he needs the company of young men his own age. Don't take that away from him."

Her expression ran through the gamut of bewilderment, annoyance and finally determination. Fascinated, Luc watched a soft blush colour her cheeks.

"There is nothing between us." Her voice was cold.

She was so wrong. Thoughts of Eva gave him a hard-on more often than he cared to acknowledge. And he knew she couldn't control her physical response to him any more than he could. Her blushes, the way she met his kisses gave her away. He smiled and leaned close, and dropped his voice to a whisper. "Liar."

She sat ramrod straight and blinked several times. "Despite what you think you know about me, we do not have a *relationship*."

"Then why did you kiss me?"

"*You* kissed me. I've never kissed you." She glared at him and wriggled in her seat. Luc swallowed a grin. Was she getting turned on by their spat as much as he was?

"I never. Oh!" Her hand shot up to cover her mouth and her eyes widened. "That's so ungentlemanly."

"I never claimed to be a gentleman. And for all your refined English ways, if you're honest, you prefer me when I'm not."

Her chest rose with indignation and he rather enjoyed the view.

"Why you arrogant—"

Luc covered her hand and circled her wrist with his fingers. "Why does your pulse race when I touch you?" Slowly, he rubbed his thumb across her knuckles.

"You've tried every which way to get hold of my plantation and you don't like not getting your way. Is it the fact I'm a woman who won't give in to you the most galling aspect? Or is it that I make you—" She cut off the rest of the sentence and picked up her cup.

He leaned closer until Eva's breath brushed across his cheek and her perfume wrapped around him. His gaze flickered lower. Her pulse beat rapidly in the hollow of her throat and her breasts rose and fell. "Make me do what? What do you want to do to me? I know what I want to do with you."

"I want to make you acknowledge that I can run my plantation as well as you run yours. And after that—"

"After that, we can have a relationship? Why wait? If we work together, we'd be a certainty to win that contract. Combine our resources, my expertise, your presentation... Seb told me about the tours you ran at Bellerose."

"If I can't do it on my own, I don't deserve to win. I have to try."

"You're not going to win that contract alone, you know. They want local experience to back up the winning application."

Gracefully she rose to her feet. "Don't be too sure. The Board will be meeting to consider *my* proposal soon." She turned on her heel and walked away, stilettos tap-tapping across the marble floor, hips swaying in fascinating rhythm as she retreated, head high.

He eased back in his seat and crossed his legs, sipped his coffee and watched her over the top of the cup. Damn the plantation, damn the contract, and damn this attraction. He wanted Eva—badly. But if it was a fight she wanted, he was the man to give it to her.

Chapter Twelve

Eva gripped the newspaper and stared in disbelief. How had she and Luc made the gossip section? Below a long-distance photo of Luc and her apparently holding hands and leaning close, the words taunted her. *Local estate owners, Lucien Martineau and English heiress, Miss Evangeline Abbott in the King Kamehameha Hotel lobby yesterday. Are two of our big plantation owners considering a merger?*

She dropped the paper on the kitchen table and pressed her hands to her temples. Was this Luc's doing? Somehow, it didn't ring true. From the first day, he'd helped her. She understood his desire for her land, even while she fought him. Land meant security and more, like Luc's program that gave so much to the community.

Merging their skills and combining their two plantations made sense. But giving up control as he'd suggested? It felt like giving in to her desire for Luc, a weakness she couldn't contemplate. Not after Timothy.

But how had word of their discussion got out? Who would benefit by leaking it to the press? She nibbled her thumbnail and read the caption again.

Seb entered the kitchen without a word and avoided meeting her eyes. He reached across and grabbed a banana from the fruit bowl. As he turned to leave his hip caught the newspaper and his hand shot out to stop it falling off the table. He paused and went still.

Eva followed his glance down to the gossip page. She reached for his arm but he shook her off. "It's not what it looks like, Seb."

"You told me I couldn't work with Luc and the boys then

you run off and meet him on the quiet." He stared at her, accusation in his eyes before he raced down the hall. The front door crashed shut behind him. Moments later, his bike engine roared as he gunned it down the driveway.

She'd done it again. How did she keep making such a mess when all she wanted was what was best for Seb?

Lunch passed without his return. By the time dinner came and went and he still hadn't shown up, Eva was beside herself with worry. Enough. Luc hadn't contacted her about the newspaper story and Seb had disappeared.

She marched into her office and dialled. It rang three times before being picked up.

"Luc, it's Eva. Have you seen the paper today? Gossip pages."

"Not usually my cup of tea. Give me a minute to look."

She gripped the hand piece and pressed it to her ear. Paper rustled on the other end of the phone followed by a soft "Shit!" and several heartbeats worth of silence.

"You didn't speak to anyone about it?" Was that anger or annoyance in his tone?

She rested her head on her free hand. "No. And Seb stormed out after he saw it. He hasn't come home."

"I'm coming over." The line went dead.

For several seconds she stared at the receiver before replacing it. Luc was coming. Why did that feel so right?

***

Luc pulled up at the foot of the steps and jumped out. Eva sat curled up at one end of the swing seat, small, vulnerable and alone. Light spilled from her office window onto the veranda, burnishing golden highlights in her hair.

He was tempted to comfort her, but he'd keep his distance or they'd not talk about the leaked proposal. As he climbed the steps, she rose and walked towards him.

"Thanks for coming. I'm worried Seb's had an accident."

She stopped just out of his reach.

"I checked with the police before I came. There haven't been any accidents reported."

Eva released her breath in a long, slow sigh. "I'm sorry about this business with Seb. I just want to—"

"To protect him. I know. We'll find him." His hand reached up to stroke her cheek before he realized he'd made the movement and she tilted her head into his touch, her cheek cool and soft. When she swayed toward him it felt natural to wrap his arms around her. Her softness melted against his hard body and his arousal rejoiced at the connection. He was determined to get to the bottom of why she pushed him away when they reached a certain level of intimacy. Something was holding her back and his gut told him it wasn't their competition.

Was it possible she felt a relationship with Luc threatened all she'd done for her nephew?

"Do you remember our discussion about Seb the night we met?"

He felt her nod before she took a step back. He missed her softness and the scent of her as soon as she stepped out of his arms. Shoving his hands in his pockets, he leaned against a post. "Young men get fired up and do silly things when they're working out where they belong. His world has been turned topsy-turvy and that photo probably made him feel like more change is coming just when he's starting to get settled."

"It's not change he fears. At least, not only that. He thinks I lied to him. About—us."

"He's an intelligent young man. Give him credit for seeing what's in front of him."

"What do you mean, what's in front of him?"

"You said he stormed out of the house after seeing the photo? Don't you think that might be it then?"

"That stupid caption. Of course he would have believed it. But there isn't anything to it. He knows he's the most important person in my life."

"But what about us, Eva?"

She wrapped her arms around her waist in the gesture he was coming to recognize meant she was stressed. He'd be damned if he'd let her close him out again.

Take a chance…

His father's words filtered through his mind. He'd rejected them out of hand and thrown himself into heavy physical work. Laying himself open to a woman, trusting her, was a bad idea. But his father was no fool; there *was* something different about Eva.

Luc swallowed the lump of dread in his throat. She wouldn't accept anything less than the truth and if he wanted to find a way forward with her, that's what he had to offer. He took a deep breath, took her hand and led her to the swing seat.

"I'm going to lay my cards on the table so you know exactly where we stand. Yes, I tried to buy your property, and when I discovered Benson had sold it to you, I was angry. I wanted this property—badly—so I could expand my work program for the boys as well as claim one of the finest plantations for my own. But that has nothing to do with this attraction I feel for you. I want you, Eva. You get under my skin and I can't think of anything other than making love to you when you're near. I'm not trying to seduce you to get your property but I do want you. There it is."

Wide-eyed, she stared at him and her lips parted. Always her lips drew him like a bee to a flower. Sweeter than honey, he hungered to taste them again. Uncomfortably aware of his growing arousal and other places he'd like her mouth to explore, he was hard-pressed not to shift under her gaze. Around Eva, he seemed to be in a permanent state of arousal.

"You don't know me. How can you—want me?"

"How can I—my God, you really don't know how desirable you are. In the restaurant, every man on the Island watched you walk into the room and every man wants to be with you."

"You want to sleep with me? Is that what you're telling me?"

"Of course I want to sleep with you. A man would have to be dead not to, but I want the chance to get to know you better, too. Will you give me that chance?"

Through the open window to her office, the phone rang. She blinked and stared at him for one emotion-charged moment before she raced through the doorway with him hot on her heels. She snatched up the phone. "Eva Abbott here… Oh, yes, he is. I'll put him on." She held out the phone. "It's your man, Samuel."

He frowned. Their fingers brushed as he took the receiver and her eyes widened at the contact.

"Boss, we got Miss Abbott's brother here. He's drunk as a skunk and rambling. Moe ain't much better. What you want us to do with him?"

"Keep him there. We'll be right over." He hung up and took her hands.

Their gazes locked, hers hopeful. "He's at your place?"

He nodded. "He is and by the sound of it he's plastered. Come on." He grabbed her hand and escorted her to the Jeep.

Eva clenched her hands in her lap, her shoulders stiff as they travelled down the road. Quiet until the car hit a bump, she turned to him and suddenly words poured from her. "How could he? Drunk? He's not of legal age."

"Easy." He reached across and covered her hands with one of his. "Let's find out what happened first. Moe's going to be in big trouble though, if he's led Seb astray."

They pulled up in front of the workers' quarters. Samuel lounged in a doorway, a cigarette dangling from his lower lip. As they climbed out of the Jeep, he ground it out and slipped it into the cuff of his jeans. "Hey, boss, Miss Abbott. Both boys have been throwing up and Seb's been rambling on 'bout lot of nonsense but he's okay now. He's gonna have one hell of a headache—pardon me, miss—tomorrow."

She stopped in front of the bunkhouse door and looked up at the big Hawaiian. "Thank you for phoning. I was quite worried about him. May I see him, please?"

"Sure thing, Miss Abbott. This way." Samuel led her into a dorm fitted with half a dozen bunks, a large table, and benches.

Luc grabbed her arm before she could cross to where Seb lay moaning on one of the lower bunks, an arm flung over his eyes. "Telling him off won't be any use tonight. Save it until his hangover has worn off."

She drew a deep breath and nodded. "Thanks."

He moved over to check on Moe in another of the bunks. The boy sprawled in a tangle of sheets, sound asleep and snoring like a buzz-cutter.

Gingerly, she sat on the edge of the bunk and touched Seb's cheek. "It's Evie. I'm going to take you home."

He groaned. His speech slurred as he squinted up at her. "Don't be mad. Didn't mean to get frunk. Showed Ben the diary. Him and me'll dig for emeralds tomorrow. Promise." He grabbed his stomach. "Gonna throw up."

Samuel thrust a bucket in between them. "'Scuse me, miss."

Eva jumped out of the way and muttered, "Why would he do that?"

Luc pulled her further away. "It's the drink talking. I wouldn't worry. Look, how about you leave him here for the night? We'll keep an eye on him for you."

"I can't impose like that."

"Someone will have to sit up with Moe anyway. It's as easy to keep an eye on two as one. You can stay up at the house, or I'll run you home if you prefer, but Seb will be better off not having to take another car ride tonight."

Her shoulders drooped.

Luc curled his hands into fists to keep from reaching for

her. The boy would have some explaining to do to him as well.

And he had a few choice words to say about doing the right thing by his aunt. One way or another, Seb wasn't going to have a pleasant day tomorrow.

Seb groaned again and Samuel grinned and turned to her. "Don't worry 'bout him, Miss. I'll keep an eye on him for you."

"Thank you, Samuel. I'll leave him in your tender care. Goodnight."

Luc followed her out of the bunkhouse to the far side of the Jeep. She leaned against the side and rested her head on her arms. "What am I doing wrong? Tell me, what more can I do?"

"Let him come back here to work. He needs company his own age and he needs stability."

"But he should be on *our* plantation. And it isn't right to keep imposing on you."

Unable to refrain from touching her, he tipped her chin up and smoothed her hair back from her brow. "I don't want his inheritance. I want you. Stay here tonight, no strings."

"After what you said earlier? Do you think it wise?" She gave him a smile that wobbled as she tried to hold it in place.

He grinned ruefully and released her. "I doubt it's wise, and I'm not saying the thought hasn't crossed my mind—a lot—but you look exhausted. I've a guest room you can use."

"Not tonight. If you don't mind me borrowing your car, I'll bring it back in the morning and save you the trip."

"No, I'll drive you home now. I'm sure I'm going to regret it though. Tell you what, how about I take you out for a joy flight tomorrow, after we've sorted out our two miscreants? I can show you some of the coastline."

Her face lit up at his offer. "Joy flight? You can fly?"

"Yep. We can head down past Diamond Head and have a picnic on a quiet little beach I know, and be back in plenty of time for your meeting. You might even enjoy yourself."

Her gaze flicked away and she caught her lip in her teeth.

"Don't over think it, Eva. Just say yes."

"Yes."

Chapter Thirteen

Luc piloted the Bell 47 helicopter along the cliffs, flying low and slower than the cruising speed they'd maintained for the first hour. Leaning over to look through her glass door, Eva could see everything. Surf crashed against the cliff base in a spray of white spume and a little way offshore, a pod of dolphins broke through the waves. She touched the microphone to her lip as he'd shown her. "It's wonderful. I've never seen anything so beautiful."

His voice crackled through her headset. "Hang on tight. We're going in to land." He navigated close to the dark grey wall of rock, skimming just above the tree line. Suddenly an opening appeared on her side of the helicopter. Framed by large boulders stepping down to the sea, the entrance to the small lagoon was invisible until they were on top of it. Fringed in white sand and lush tropical bushes, the lagoon was protected and calm.

Luc set down gently on the only wide section of beach and turned off the rotors. They slowed with a *thump-thump*. When they stopped whirring, she removed her headset and ran her fingers through her hair. He jumped out and came around to open her door. Hands warm through the material of her sarong, he lifted her out.

"Wow! That was some ride."

"You handled it like a trooper."

"And this is beautiful." She turned in a slow, sweeping circle.

"Welcome to paradise. Choose a place to set up. It's a tidal lagoon so not too close to the water." He grinned. "Unless you want to eat *in* the water?"

Eva stepped out of her sandals and dropped them inside the helicopter. Slipping an arm under her hair she lifted it off her neck, thanking her lucky stars for the latest fashion in bathing suits. The high-backed halter neck was fashionable and hid her scars. Tightening the knot of her sarong about her waist, she slipped her sunglasses on and set off up the beach.

Heat warmed the soles of her feet as she wandered along the fringe of pure white sand. After the break in and the fire and her struggles with Seb, it was heavenly to put aside her responsibilities for one day. Luc came up behind her carrying a wicker picnic hamper with a tartan blanket balanced on top. "Where do you want to eat?"

"How about over beside that little waterfall? It's shady but far enough away from the coconut trees that I won't lose my pilot to a falling nut."

"Good thinking." He deposited the hamper on the sand, picked up the blanket, and shook it open. "So, food first or swim?"

"I'm pretty hot after that flight. How about a swim? I took your advice."

"Wow, there's a first time for everything." Hands on hips, he grinned at her. "And which piece of advice would that be?"

Ignoring his jibe, she kneeled in front of the picnic hamper and unbuckled the leather straps. She took out a flask of water, poured two cups, and offered him one. "I'm already wearing my swimsuit. If we swim before we eat, we'll dry off by the time we leave."

He raised his cup in a silent toast.

Until now, she hadn't considered how exposed she would feel in the form-fitting, fine wool swimwear. Slowly, she untied the knot on her sarong. Luc's gaze followed her movements as the long ties fell open and she grabbed at the material, clasping it to her waist. Conscious of his amused expression, she fiddled with the neck of her new bathing suit and tugged the neckline higher.

Butterflies fluttered in her stomach at the thought of revealing so much more of her body. It wasn't that he undressed her with his eyes, exactly, but more like he saw through whatever armour she wrapped herself in.

She raised an eyebrow in query. "Well, what do you prefer?"

"Your reasoning is flawless. Swim it is." He hauled off his shirt and dropped it on the blanket.

Eva stared, unable to tear her gaze from his body. Bronzed and bare-chested, Luc in swimming trunks surpassed Charles Atlas—in every way. Muscles rippled beneath golden-tanned skin. Broad shoulders tapered to a narrow waist and a line of dark hair arrowed down from his stomach and was lost beneath his trunks.

It didn't matter what he wore—or didn't—he was the most mouth-watering male she'd ever seen.

Hands on hips, his dark eyes challenged her. "You might want to lose the sarong and leave your sunglasses on the beach."

She licked her lips. "Yes, of course. My glasses." She turned her back and dropped the sarong then the glasses on top of it. All she had to do was walk nonchalantly into the water and stroke out a little way. She adjusted the fashionably wide *faux* belt of her swimsuit—impractical but pretty—and smoothed her palms over her hips.

Breathe and walk. She managed three steps toward the lagoon.

Without warning, Luc scooped her into his arms and ran into the water, splashing her with cold droplets that sizzled on her heated skin. The sandy bottom fell away and they plunged off a ledge into cool, blue depths. She squealed, the sound cut off as water closed over her head. Instinctively, she grabbed at his shoulders.

Streams of silver bubbles rose around their heads and burst where they caught in tumbles of auburn hair. Light rippled in waves across his face and chest. They rolled in a half turn, like lazy seals in the North Sea. Sunlight blinded her. In the watery brightness Luc's arm clamped around her waist and their legs tangled.

He pushed off the sandy bottom and they burst through the surface.

She wrapped one arm around his neck as she brushed curls off her face and gulped in air. Luc grinned, and her pulse quickened at the gleam in his eyes. She pushed away from his chest, flipped around and sent a wave of water at him. Caught by surprise, he spluttered and shook his head. Droplets of water arced into the air around him, shimmering with trapped sunlight before they splattered back.

"Payback for the dunking," she called and quickly stroked towards the waterfall.

For the first time since forever, a sense of lightness and freedom filled Eva and laughter bubbled from her lips. She floated onto a ledge under the waterfall, flung her arms wide, and tipped her head back. Eyes closed, she let the water pour over her face and body.

The rush of water was broken by Luc's deep laughter as he pulled her off her perch into deeper water. She draped her arms loosely about his neck. Hard and inviting, his erection rose between them, pressing into her stomach. Each breath she inhaled rubbed her breasts against his chest and her nipples pebbled with awareness.

Their gazes meshed and his dark eyes deepened, blazing with desire. Slowly, he sculled back until they reached waist-deep water. He turned so she was standing in the shallows. A droplet rolled down the side of his face and she leaned in, caught it on her tongue and retraced its path up his cheek. He drew a sharp breath and buried his face in her shoulder. His lips traced their own path up her neck and along her jaw to the corner of her mouth.

Just a fraction of an inch away lay paradise. She flung both arms around his neck and wrapped her legs around his waist. Positioned over his straining erection, heat bloomed between her thighs, intense and inevitable.

Eva turned her head and pressed her mouth to his.

Hands cupping her bottom, Luc carried her out of the water to the blanket and kneeled at the edge. Perched in his lap, she wriggled closer. He slipped his fingers into the tangled mass of her wet hair, his thumbs stroking her cheeks as his tongue invaded her mouth. His hands moved round her head and his fingers brushed the buttons on her halter neck. He slipped the first undone.

Something niggled in her brain but the thought was elusive as his mouth captured hers. A second button popped open. His fingers brushed her neck—her bare neck—and she shuddered at the deliciousness of his touch on her skin. The firm fit of her wool-knit bathing suit loosened. She moved her head and her tangled hair caught on a button. The tug pulled her out of her dreamy state to full awareness. Luc was undressing her. One more button and he'd feel and see the scars she'd hidden for so long.

She wrenched her mouth from his and pushed backwards off his lap. "No, Luc. Don't, please."

His eyes flew open, and he frowned. "What's wrong?"

"I can't—you mustn't—I—" Tears pricked her eyes and she tipped her head back, refusing to let them fall. How could she forget where she was and whom she was with?

He reached out to touch her and she held out a hand to stop him. He dropped his hand to his thigh, his fingers curling into a fist, muscles tensed with leashed power. "I thought we both wanted this. Was I wrong?"

He was oh, so right. She wanted him like he couldn't imagine. She gulped down her despair and the longing for him that could never be. "I'm sorry if I misled you, Luc. I'm—not good at relationships." Under the mass of wet curls, she fumbled, seeking the buttons of her suit. Damn the buttons and damn her for being a fool. What had she expected, coming here with him today?

"Correct me if I'm wrong but I thought we were both enjoying that kiss. What am I missing here?" His voice was soft and controlled but she recognized the effort he was making to understand her abrupt refusal. Perhaps she had deserved her ex-beau's insults.

She gave up searching for the buttons and ran both hands over her hair, smoothing it into place. Somehow she had to slip back into her mask, the one she presented to the rest of the world. The one that said nothing and no one could touch her, while on the inside her stomach flipped and clenched.

Poor Luc. No wonder he was puzzled at the mixed signals she was sending. "Look, what is it they say in those American movies? 'It's not you, it's me.' Well, it is me, Luc. I'm little Miss Frigidaire. You don't want to tangle with me because you'll get frostbite." She tried, God how she tried, to keep the bitterness out of her voice. After all this time, her ex-fiancé's label still had the power to hurt.

His gaze narrowed on her face and it was all she could do not to squirm under that concentrated appraisal. "Liar."

She pressed her clasped hands to her lips and drew a slow breath to steady herself. The truth couldn't be ignored or glossed over any longer. She lied to Luc by offering what she couldn't give him. And she'd lied to herself when she thought she could be with him like this and have nothing happen. Truth was she'd wanted it to happen but it hurt more than she expected to hear him call her on it. Softly, she answered him. "That's the second time you've called me that."

"Because you are. You're not an ice queen. You put on a mask to hide the real you but by God, woman, in my arms you're heat and passion. There's not one damned thing about you that's cold."

He was right. In his arms, she was that woman and together they were incendiary. "I'm sorry."

"You're hiding scars that you don't you want the world to see."

So gentle, his tone. So inviting to confide her darkest fears and share the burden of her disfigurement. And then what? A happy-ever-after because he felt sorry for her? Sympathy sex was not an option.

"You know about the scars—I mean—" Words deserted her.

He frowned and when she dared peek at him, his eyes were fixed on her face. "I was talking about emotional scars from the loss of your family but that's not what you mean, is it?"

She drew a shaky breath and shook her head. "No." Her voice emerged in a whisper, all but lost on the breeze that rippled across the lagoon. Escape was impossible but she needed to get away from Luc and his damned *caring* tone. She surged to her feet. Luc grabbed her hand and tugged her back into his arms.

"Stop running, Eva. Whatever your demons, let me help you face them."

"Let me go." She pushed against his chest.

He wrapped his arms more tightly around her. "I'm not letting go until you answer me. Is that why you wear your hair down all the time? To hide a scar?"

"None of your damned business." She bucked and wriggled in vain. His hold on her would not be broken. Oh, God, the irony of it wasn't lost on her.

"You hide behind your hair in more ways than one. Why?"

Persistent, insufferable man. His determination to wrest long-buried secrets from her cracked her resolve.

"You want to know—really?" She eased an arm free from his hold. "This is why." Defiantly, she tugged her hair to one side and turned her back to him. With fingers that trembled on the last button, she flicked it undone.

And waited.

The iron band around her heart tightened as she waited for his gasp of horror, his withdrawal from her damaged self. She pressed her lips together. He would not see her cry.

Resolutely, she kept her back to him and spoke over her shoulder so she didn't have to see his disgust or, worse, his sympathy. It didn't matter which now. "I had a fiancé who dumped me faster than you can say Christopher Robin when he learned all he'd gotten for his bargain was an imperfect me and not the manor house. What's the matter? Have I struck you dumb?"

"No. But why cover it up?"

"It's hideous." She reached back to draw the edges of her suit together.

Luc's hands covered hers, foiling her attempt. He shifted closer behind her, his breath puffing past her ear. "It's part of who you are. You're a survivor and you are a beautiful woman."

Feather-light, his mouth touched her scarred back in a kiss that stole her breath and shocked her to her core. Eyes closed, Eva tipped her head to accommodate him. He wrapped his hands around her shoulders and eased her onto his lap. Soft lips moved an inch higher and kissed her again, his breath cool across her damp skin. The tenderness of his touch threatened to spill her tears.

He trailed his fingers over her bare skin and unwound a curl that had snagged around the buttons then slipped her strap off one shoulder. "I want you, Eva." Low and sexy, his voice sent a shiver down her spine. Gently, he turned her to face him.

Her gaze travelled up his face, from his firm jaw to lips that could make her forget the rest of the world. She searched for signs of sympathy, anything that would tell her this wasn't real. Long lashes framed chocolate-brown eyes afire with lust and longing.

For me? Yearning for Luc filled her, a wanting so deep, so fierce it was all she could do not to reach for him. Years of hiding and humiliation made it hard to give up the notion that any man could want her. Especially a man like Luc. "How can you bear to look let alone touch—me?"

"It's a mark that you survived. Did it happen during the war?"

Struggling with survivor guilt had been a constant for so long that his perspective turned her self image on its head. Disconcerting, it was also oddly comforting. She nodded. "A bomb in the heart of London killed my parents and Phillip's wife. I'd gone out the back of the restaurant to the ladies toilet. The bomb that killed them blew the door off the outhouse. Luckily for me, because the roof was on fire. It caved in on me but I was pulled free although not quickly enough to prevent the burns on my back. I had months of operations and rehabilitation before the doctors said there was no more they could do."

She closed her eyes as memory swirled back, the noise and confusion, sirens and smoke. And the rats fleeing the nearby sweets factory. And agonizing weeks lying on her front when any touch was torture.

Softly, he cupped her cheek, his touch banishing the painful memories. His voice recalled her to the present and soothed an ache she'd carried far too long. "I'm sorry for your losses, but you can't let that guilt ruin your life or stop you being intimate. You are a very beautiful woman and your scar is part of who you are. You deserve to be loved and I want to make love to you. Now."

No longer wanting or able to hide, she opened her eyes. He kneeled before her and he was real and glorious and he desired her.

"Eva?"

Every hidden desire she'd ever craved was wrapped up in Luc. "Yes."

She melted into his arms. His mouth claimed hers in a kiss like she'd never known. Nerve ends tingled beneath his touch and her wanton body, starved of a lover's touch, clamoured for skin on skin contact. With a tenderness at odds with the demands of his lips on hers, he eased her onto the blanket and lowered himself over her. He drew back a little and she missed his body heat as he rested on his forearms and waited until she opened her eyes. "Do you trust me, Eva?"

Lost in lust, it took several heartbeats to register what he was asking. Did she trust him?

"If you've got any doubts tell me now because soon I won't be able to stop."

She looked into his face and saw desire and tenderness, saw

Luc, who had been there for her and Seb from the beginning. He'd been there when she needed him and he was here now, needing her, wanting to make love to her. *With* her.

"No doubts, Luc. Make love to me."

He donned protection and then he kissed her lips, trailed kisses down her neck, along the neckline of her bathing suit. Easing it off her shoulders, his mouth explored every inch of her body until she could take no more. The ridge of his erection pressed against her thigh, steel covered in satin, hard against her softness. Her last coherent thought before she imploded was to take him into her body. "Now, I need you, now."

"Thank, God." He pulled her leg around his hip and entered in one hard thrust, groaning as her tight sheath welcomed him. He filled her body and soul, and she felt beautiful.

***

Eva gathered the sarong to her chest, passed the length behind her and back to the front. Two quick twists of the ends around one another and she knotted it behind her neck.

"Like Dorothy Lamour in the *Road* movies." Luc chuckled and tugged her into his arms. His expression became serious. "Promise me you won't hide anymore? Don't let how you think others might react dictate how you live your life."

"Right now, I feel like I could conquer a mountain."

He kissed her slowly, his lips soft and sweet like spring rain and rested his forehead against hers. "Much as I don't want to, we need to leave. This helicopter's not equipped for flying at night and you have a meeting to catch. Come on."

He took her hand and stepped off the blanket, stooped and grabbed one end. "Mind your eyes." He moved downwind from her and shook it.

She scooped the barely touched picnic food into the hamper and watched the muscles in his back as he folded the blanket. Her mouth curved into an involuntary smile. Picnicking on Luc would make any day better.

He turned and their gazes met. He must have sensed the direction of her thoughts. A low growl erupted from him and purred right through her. "Keep looking at me like that, woman, and we might not be leaving here tonight."

Warmth rushed into her cheeks and her breath caught in her throat. *Yes, please.*

"Eva, I'm serious. I'm within an inch of making love to you again. Is that what you want? To spend the night here on the beach with me?"

"I'm willing."

A muscle spasmed in his cheek and his Adam's apple bobbed up and down. He folded his arms across his still bare chest. "But I'm not. Think of your reputation."

"Then put on your *damned* shirt and stop tormenting me."

"Is that all it takes to turn you on? I must remember for next time." He donned his shirt, taking his sweet time to adjust it around his shoulders. Still unbuttoned, he looked across at her and grinned. "Better?"

She strolled across the sand and stopped in front of him, her body close but not quite touching his. Bare chest beckoned and she traced a pathway down the centre to his belly button.

A whorl of dark hair surrounded it and continued beneath the waistband of his swimming trunks. Pausing at his navel, she walked her fingers around the edge then snapped the band of his trunks. "Two can play at that game, Luc. Remember *that*."

With a toss of her head she turned and sashayed away in her best imitation of Dorothy Lamour. "Are you coming?"

"Retribution will be so sweet." If the low rumble of his voice was any indication, their next encounter promised to be very sweet. Her body thrummed in expectation and she understood the appeal of Mae West's characters. It was a pity they had to leave just as she learned to spread her wings.

"Big talk," she called over her shoulder and headed up the beach. Near their landing spot, her foot scraped against a solid object in the sand. A small conch, perfect in shape and colouring, lay partially revealed. She picked it up and shook it. Pale pink inside and with a fluted lip, it would sit on her desk at home, a beautiful reminder of a perfect day.

As she strolled back to the chopper, Luc slung the hamper and blanket behind his seat and secured them. He checked his watch and turned to the sea beyond the lagoon. "We'd better get underway. As it is, we'll be cutting it fine to get back for your meeting. Are you ready?"

She nodded and climbed into her seat. He shut her door and walked around to his side, then stopped and frowned, lifting his head.

"What is it? Is something wrong?"

"I've got to check underneath." He disappeared below the helicopter.

Eva jumped onto the sand and kneeled beside him. "What's that wet patch near your elbow? And that smell. Is this machine supposed to smell like that?"

"No." He ran his fingers along a length of tubing, stopped and leaned closer to examine it. His brow crinkled and his eyes narrowed at the length of tube in his hands. He ran a finger around where it joined the body of the engine and rubbed his thumb and finger together. "This hose looks like it's been tampered with. There's a slit up close to the tank that's allowed oil to seep out as the engine cooled."

"Where? Show me." Eva wriggled in closer.

"It's a fine, clean cut. Most likely made with a knife."

A knife making sparks on a whetstone. A blade tossed in the air and deftly caught.

As the images flashed through her mind she sucked in a breath and gagged on the stink of aviation fuel. She pushed backwards, banged her head on a metal strut and fell onto a patch of damp sand. Stomach churning, she stumbled several yards into the bushes. Damn it, she was not going to throw up in front of Luc.

Leaves rustled behind her and his hand rested on her shoulder. He squeezed it gently, reassuring her by simple touch that he was there for her. "Are you okay?"

Hands pressed to her stomach, she turned and faced him. "The smell. It got to me. I'm okay now."

Except for the fact of a knife-cut to their oil line. Deliberate and calculated to ensure that, one way or another, they didn't return home. Was it intended to kill them or to delay them and buy someone time? To do what?

"Am I being paranoid or has the helicopter been sabotaged?"

His gaze rested on hers and a frown formed between his brows.

"I'm a big girl. I can cope with whatever it is you're thinking." At least, she could cope while Luc was around to wrap her in his arms and keep the world at bay.

"Honestly? I can't see how that damage could be anything but deliberate."

"Do you think we were meant to crash?" Heart thudding painfully in her chest, breath trapped in her lungs, she waited for his answer. Did someone want them—*her*—dead? Who knew they were flying today, aside from their families and their workers? "I told Seb and Stefan where we were going but no one else."

Luc took her into his arms and stroked her hair off her face. His touch released something inside and she sagged against him. In his arms, nothing bad would happen. All she had to do was stay there forever. "I doubt it. Whoever cut that line didn't want us returning in a hurry though. If we'd flown on to the volcano first we might have had to make an emergency landing. I'm rather glad we decided to stop here for our picnic." He kissed her forehead.

"So, cut oil line, eh?"

A ghost of a grin softened the stern line of his lips. "Would you believe we've run out of gas?"

"And I thought that only happened in the movies."

"We're not going to get back tonight. I'm sorry."

"We're safe and help will come soon." She reached up and stroked the side of his face. Five o'clock shadow bristled under her touch. What would it feel like on that sensitive skin between her thighs? "Will anyone come looking for us? I mean, when we don't return by sunset."

"They won't be able to do anything until morning. There's no helicopter capable of making night flights at the airport. And the rock walls around the lagoon mean we can't radio out either. We're here for the night."

"But you logged a flight plan, didn't you?"

"Someone will be here in the morning."

Her body exulted in the knowledge. They were safe. While the thought of what might have happened was scary, she had a whole night with Luc. "Then it's a good thing we've got plenty of food. Do you want to drag out that hamper and blanket again? We're going to need them."

"Good idea. We'll set up camp where we had lunch." He released her and turned to look beyond the opening of the lagoon.

She followed his gaze. Whitecaps sparkled in late afternoon sunlight while around their sleepy lagoon, shadows lengthened.

"Gather whatever wood you can find. I'm going to set off a flare from the rocks on the beach, just in case any late flights are heading in. I won't be long." He pulled out the emergency kit from the helicopter, removed a flare and tucked a box of matches into his shirt pocket. Grim-faced, he frowned, and then added a knife to his stash before heading off through the opening to the beach.

Goose bumps marched down her arms and Eva shivered. Seeing the knife in his hands brought memories of the bad things that had happened crashing around her.

Until that moment, she'd considered the lagoon a paradise on earth. Luc's action shattered the illusion. Unwilling to venture too far from the beach, she made her way through the trees on a parallel track with the shore. Shadows deepened and lengthened while she collected an armful of fallen twigs and small branches. Treading carefully to avoid stepping on rocks in her bare feet, she made her way back to their abandoned picnic spot.

Off to the right, something rustled in the bushes. She held her breath as her gaze darted to the side. Slowly, she bent her knees and deposited her load of firewood on the ground. One branch, sturdier than the rest offered her best form of defence. Taking shallow breaths, she held the wood in front of her at arms' length and stepped forward.

Leaves rustled and soft, stealthy footfalls came closer. Eyes wide, she gripped her weapon and raised her arms above her head.

"What are you doing, Eva?"

She screamed and swung her stick.

Luc grabbed her wrists and pulled her against him. The hard length of his body was a haven but his face swam through her blurred vision. "There was something moving in the bushes. I thought—"

"You thought you'd turn hunter and catch our dinner." He nodded his head at the bush. "Do you know what you were stalking?"

"What?" Bemused by the gleam in his eyes, she forced herself to look over her shoulder.

A large ground-dwelling bird strutted around the bush, pecked at a fallen nut, and eyed her with apparent disdain for her attempts to hunt it. The brown bird emitted a throaty call, pecked at the nut once more and strutted off through the greenery.

"I must be more unnerved than I realized. Poor bird."

He chuckled and dropped a swift kiss on her lips. "I'm pretty impressed but I don't think you want to try cooking one of those. Come on, let's get a fire going. It will get quite cool as the sun goes down."

***

She pushed up onto her elbows to watch as Luc hunkered down and threw another branch on the fire. A shower of sparks drifted into the dark sky amid a thin stream of spiralling smoke and winked out somewhere above his head. Outlined by the campfire's glow, he adjusted the position of the wood and dusted off his hands. He moved back, dropped down beside her, and casually wrapped an arm around her shoulders.

Night breezes blew strands of hair across her face and raised goose bumps down her arm. "You were right about the temperature dropping at night. Thank goodness for the fire and the blanket."

He wrapped his other arm around her and ran his hand up and down her exposed skin. "Shared body warmth is much more effective. Basic survival technique 101."

"I'm willing to share some heat." Goodness, did that sound forward, wanton even? She bit her lip and heat rose in her face. But the thought of making love again with Luc was tempting. Why try to resist something so good? Even the sabotage of their helicopter couldn't dim her anticipation.

She turned her head. Golden skin filled her vision, the column of his throat, the expanse of his bare chest through his unbuttoned shirt. She touched her lips to his skin. Salty. She licked her lips and kissed him again, right where his pulse beat. It sped up under the pressure of her lips and a little thrill raced through her at her ability to stir him.

His arms tightened about her and his chest swelled as he sucked in and held a breath. "Remember what I said?"

She drew back a little and tipped her head to look into his eyes. "About what?"

He leaned close and his lips brushed her ear. "Retribution." *Oh.*

Soft and seductive, his voice promised sweet heaven. And his lips—he kissed the edge of her mouth. Flutters trembled through her stomach and she closed her eyes. His tongue traced her upper lip and she held her breath. Her secret place throbbed and she squeezed her thighs together.

Sweet retribution. She must remember to stir him more often.

His hand slid down to her hip, circled, massaged, and cupped her bottom. He changed position, taking her with him until she lay beneath his body on the blanket.

She opened her eyes. Stars whirled above his head and a half moon hung low on the horizon, casting a soft light on one side of his face.

He leaned in, blocking out the starlight, his breath warm across her cheek. Soft kisses whispered over her eyelids, her nose, her cheeks, and his voice murmured against her ear. "So sweet."

She ached for the same touch and turned her head, trying to catch his mouth.

He chuckled and straddled her, rocking lightly. Pressure increased on her mound. She gasped and relinquished her embrace on his neck. Her hands clenched on the blanket. Heat flowed through her body, pulsing from her core with each slow tilt of his hips. She pressed up, lifting her hips to meet his.

He placed a finger on her lips and shook his head. Light as a feather, he ran both hands down the sensitive inside skin of her arms. When he reached her wrists, his thumbs brushed over her rapidly beating pulse. Suddenly, he grasped both wrists in one hand and drew her arms above her head. He kissed the corner of her mouth and across her cheek. He stopped and gently bit her ear lobe, nuzzled the sensitive skin behind and traced her ear.

Her sarong slid up her thighs and fell open as he moved over her. Without her damp swimsuit, she lay open and exposed to him. His hips and chest held her immobile. Skin on skin. She was at his mercy. Delicious languor filled her, anticipation, and acceptance of whatever he chose to do to her. *Retribution.*

Her eyes fluttered open. Giving up control to Luc was strangely liberating. She ran her tongue over her upper lip, hoping his mouth would follow suit.

A wicked gleam sparked in his eyes and he grinned, his

gaze focused on her mouth. The rocking motion ceased and he laughed softly. "I'm enjoying this."

"Kiss me."

"I haven't finished tasting you." His fingers slipped around the back of her neck, untied her sarong, and slipped the material down. Exposed to night air and his hungry gaze, her nipples peaked. "Now—"

He bent his head and ran his tongue over the swell of her breasts, circled her nipples and flicked them. She shivered at the touch of cool air along the damp trail, a reminder, if she needed one, of his promise to taste her all over. It was so erotic, so provocatively shocking. And she loved it.

A lock of hair tickled her chin as he bent his head again but now his mouth closed around one nipple and sucked. Hard.

Electric pulses ran from her breast directly to her womb, setting fire to every nerve along the way. She gasped and arched up.

He kissed her nipple and gently scraped his stubbled chin in the valley between her breasts. "You're so responsive, Eva. It's like you've never been made love to before."

Pecks on the cheek and a quick, painful tumble with her fiancé in the music room after his proposal—*to seal the deal*, his words, not hers—didn't qualify. There wasn't the remotest connection between that and bliss like she'd never known. She struggled to shape words when her whole body was absorbed in just being, on feeling. "I haven't, not like this."

He cocked an eyebrow at her and sat up, released his hold on her wrists and straddled her hips again. "Darling, if you think that felt good, trust me, you'll enjoy what follows."

Trust him? She'd literally put herself in his hands. She giggled at the thought.

Happiness was too elusive not to grasp what he offered. She wriggled a little beneath him and reached out to touch the bulge of his erection straining through his swimwear.

He stopped her hand reaching its destination by picking it up and dropping a kiss into the palm. His lips brushed over the skin of her inside wrist. Such an innocent kiss but her legs turned to jelly at his touch. In the flickering firelight, he met and held her eyes as he slid slowly backwards.

"Hmm, let's see what this does." He lowered his head to her belly button, circled and licked and gently nipped the skin around it. Each nip telegraphed his desire and built her hunger for more. Under his ministrations she squirmed. Stubble rasped across her belly, her muscles contracted, and she felt his mouth curve into a smile against her skin. "Two can play at this game. Retribution, remember?"

Retribution. So excruciatingly sweet and erotic she could hardly breathe. "When do I get to play?"

"You don't. Not yet." As though they had all the time in the world, he returned to stroking her skin with tongue and lips, tasting, kissing, *teasing*. And then he spread her legs and kissed her, there. In that shocking, private *sweet* place, his tongue lapped her essence.

A whimper rose in her throat and she struggled to fill her lungs against the desire blooming through her body, filling her from that place between her thighs until there was no room for anything as trivial as air to breathe.

Luc slipped a finger inside and his thumb circled the spot where his tongue had driven her mad with need.

"Oh, God, Luc, I want—I need—"

"I know." He withdrew his finger. She wanted to cry out at the loss but he covered her mouth with his. Instead, their two scents combined as she tasted her essence on his lips and tongue. The taste of sex.

He deepened the kiss and their tongues tangoed.

He lifted his head. His eyes were dark, except where the fire reflected in his pupils. "Are you ready for me?"

Ready? She'd been ready from the moment she fell in his

arms. "Yes." Her response was barely a word, more of a breathy sigh of need and want and lust-filled desire.

He eased into her slowly, letting her adjust to his size, withdrew slowly and then pushed in further. When she thought she couldn't take any more, he increased the tempo, thrusting harder, faster, stronger. Pleasure blossomed through her like a flower. No more than a collection of nerve endings on fire for her lover, she cried aloud her pleasure to the night and the stars. Dimly she was aware of him following her.

Buried deep within her, he rolled onto his back taking her with him.

A delicious lethargy overtook Eva. Incapable of movement, she sprawled across his chest, hair fanned over his shoulder. Below her cheek, his heart thumped in time with hers. Wrapped in his embrace, she felt truly beautiful for the first time in her life.

His fingers lazily traced a path along her arm and across her back. Her scarred back that he'd kissed and now caressed. Her sight blurred and she blinked, her lashes brushing his chest. Happy tears. She pressed her lips to his skin and snuggled closer as he covered them with the blanket.

His lips brushed her temple, soft and sweet, and he smoothed her hair off her face. "That should have been your first time."

Chapter Fourteen

Morning sun gilded the ocean and clouds hung low and puffy on the horizon. It was too early for a spotter plane to be up but Luc needed time alone to think. He jumped from the rocks at the entrance to the lagoon onto white sand and strode along the narrow stretch of beach. Where high tide lapped at vegetation he sloshed through water, uncaring if he soaked his clothes.

Last night with Eva had been a revelation. The closed woman of previous weeks, the one who both attracted and maddened him, enticed and at times shut him out, had blossomed before his eyes into a wild, magnificent lover. Cool seawater swirled around his knees but his body reacted to the memory of her moving beneath him, of her taste on his lips and her scent. He'd woken beside her in the early dawn light and lay watching her sleep in his arms. In the bliss of sleep, worries and cares forgotten, her face was serene until she snuggled her delectable body into his. Her breasts brushed his chest and her legs tangled with his. Her hips wriggled, pressing her mound against his fully formed erection, and she made that little mewling sound like just before she came last night. He'd wanted to bury himself in her again.

Instead, he'd eased out of the blanket and her embrace and headed for the beach. Shading his eyes, he scanned the canopy of blue.

With Eva, it had been more than just having sex. He'd asked for her trust and she'd given it. Not something she did easily. He savoured the luxury of that trust, of her giving nature. In spite of their negotiation for her land, she had trusted him with herself and opened up to him. Perhaps there was a chance for them after all. His heart thudded at the thought of a future he'd given up on.

And then he remembered. How could he have been so

stupid? What if she was pregnant after last night? His jaw tightened. Why hadn't he brought more condoms?

I hoped for a chance with her but didn't expect to stay the night with her body snuggling into mine.

Why hadn't he pulled out that last time before it was too late? Bringing a baby into the world was the last thing he wanted but beating himself up over his carelessness was worse than useless. Like shutting the gate after the horse had bolted. But damn if she hadn't bewitched him.

A high wall of rock reared up in front of him. Waves crashed into its base and sent spumes of water arcing into the air. He shoved his hands in his pockets and turned back the way he'd come. If there was a baby, he'd convince Eva to marry him. In the meantime, he needed to keep his pants on and his trousers zipped. If there wasn't a baby, they'd have had a narrow escape and he'd court her properly. If she'd let him.

Lost in his dark thoughts, he reached the lagoon inlet all too soon. Like a mermaid, Eva was sitting on a flattish rock, legs tucked beneath her, finger-combing her tangled curls and humming softly. When she saw him she stopped mid-tangle, her smile shy and seductive at the same time.

"Good morning. You were up bright and early. I've put out the last of our food for breakfast."

His body hardened, ready for her, and he gritted his teeth. "Thanks. Thought I'd keep an eye out for the spotter plane. Shouldn't be long now." Even to his own ears his tone sounded dismissive, distant. He fisted his hands in his pockets and planted his feet in the sand.

Her smile wavered and uncertainty crept into her green eyes. She pressed her lips together and ducked her head, hiding behind the curtain of her hair.

Surely she could understand how much talk there would be? If he didn't handle it carefully, her reputation would be tarnished. By him.

"Regardless of the fact our chopper was sabotaged it won't do you any good that we spent the night together. There'll be talk, lots of it. We can't give the rumour mill more fodder by behaving any differently to how we have up to yesterday. Do you understand, Eva?"

She bit her lower lip. "You're saying we behave as though last night didn't happen?"

"That's right. Like nothing happened."

She straightened her shoulders and a creamy swell of breast pushed over her sarong. What he wouldn't give to tug it from her body, lay her across the rock and make love to her again now. He swallowed. And wouldn't that be a great view to greet their rescuers? A sure way to rip her reputation to pieces.

"Can you put on the rest of your clothes before rescue arrives?"

With a mumbled response he couldn't make out, she climbed swiftly off the rock and raced back to their campsite.

His brain whirred through possibilities but there was only one way he could think of to make things right for her. And the sooner he convinced her of it, the better for both of them.

Sleeping with Luc looked like it might turn out to be the worst mistake of her life. For all his talk about behaving as though the magical night they'd shared hadn't happened once rescue arrived, he'd barely spoken and when he did, he was off-handed and brusque. As though demons chased him, he'd packed their gear quickly and stowed non-personal belongings in their helicopter. No sentimentality about their beautiful night or the fact she'd opened herself to him.

Trust him? As far as she could throw him. How could she have been so foolish, especially after Timothy's betrayal?

Throughout the return flight he chatted with the rescue crew and all but ignored her. It was as though they were no more than casual strangers. In the back of her mind ran his reference to her reputation. Did he really think acting like that would stop the old biddies having a field day and bandying her name around? Never mind there were two of them on that beach; the only one to lose standing in the community would be her.

One or two of the men cast speculative glances at her until she found it easier to close her eyes and pretend to doze off behind her sunglasses.

As soon as the rescue flight landed back at base, Eva gathered her things and bolted. Deep, anonymous shade beckoned from within the hangar as she hurried across the tarmac.

Maybe they'd let her phone for a taxi from their office. It was money she didn't have to spare but anything was preferable to being in Luc's company another second.

"Eva, wait."

The sound of his voice spurred her on. She raced into the open hangar, weaved around several plane wings, and dived through a door into a small reception area.

"Evie! What happened? I was so worried when you didn't come home last night." Seb's hands dug into her shoulders and he grabbed her in a bear hug.

In the drama and joy of yesterday, she hadn't given much thought to how Seb might take the news. She slid her arms around his waist and patted him on the back. "I'm fine. It's all okay but take me home now, please."

He released her and stepped back, his gaze running over her from head to toe. Shadows under his eyes told their own story of his fear for her. "What about—?" He flicked a glance over her shoulder.

Desperate to escape before Luc caught up with her, she tugged on his arm. "Later. I'll tell you about it in the car on the way home. You can drive. Just—"

"Eva. Didn't you hear me calling you?"

The door behind her clanged shut, trapping her in the room with Luc. She sucked in a deep breath, held it, and composed herself before facing him. Neutral mask firmly in place, she turned. "Thank you for the flight, Luc. The coastline is beautiful and the picnic was lovely. Oh, and don't worry about—what happened. I don't hold you responsible—for any of it."

His eyes narrowed and he flicked a glance at Seb hovering protectively by her side. "We really need to talk."

"Funny, you seemed disinclined to talk this morning when we had plenty of time."

He moved a couple of steps closer and his hand clenched on the straps of his pack, the knuckles whitening. "There were too many ears listening."

Perhaps he was right about the flight home. If the covert speculation of the rescue crew was anything to judge by, his behaviour toward her had probably allayed some suspicion about their night together. But this morning at the lagoon he'd been so distant, like he'd got what he wanted. It would have been insulting if she hadn't felt so foolish about her participation in last night's amorous adventure.

She tilted her head a little higher. "There was plenty of opportunity before we were rescued. No matter. I'm sure the authorities will sort out the incident." She took Seb's arm and turned to the exit.

"You'll have to provide a statement. They'll need to know what's happened on your plantation. Any of it could be relevant to the—incident."

"I'll phone them tomorrow and make an appointment but I'm leaving now. As you can see, Seb is here to take me home. Thanks for the flight. It was an education." Straight back and head high, she headed out the door, praying Seb wouldn't linger and Luc wouldn't follow.

Time apart was necessary if she was to sift through the confusion of feelings whirling in her brain. She climbed in the car and slumped in her seat.

Seb put her bag in the trunk then slid behind the wheel.

"Okay, Evie, spill the beans. What *incident*? What happened out there? Do I need to knock his block off?"

"What? Oh, no, Seb, nothing like that." She made a fuss of searching for a handkerchief in her handbag.

"Why did you stay overnight with him? Because it's a damn poor show on his part if the helicopter didn't break down."

"It did. At least—" Ignorance could be dangerous. At least if he knew what had happened, he could take precautions. "The oil line was deliberately cut. We weren't meant to make it back last night."

His jaw dropped. "Who'd do a thing like that?"

"I think *why* is the more important question. Let's get home so I can shower and then we'll put our heads together and see if we can't come up with an answer."

But by evening they were none the wiser. Seb lounged in one of the Adirondack chairs on the front veranda. "It makes no sense. You and Luc could have been killed. Who would gain by that?"

She yawned. Too little sleep and too much adrenaline over the past twenty-four hours and she was limp as a dishrag. "Frankly, at this moment I'm too tired to care. What did you do last night?"

He looked shamefaced and didn't answer immediately. "It took a while before we realized you and Luc hadn't come back. I thought you might have stopped off in town for dinner."

"We? Were you over with the boys at Luc's?"

"Don't be cross. We had a poker game going. Not for money," he hurriedly added.

She suppressed her grin, pleased that he was demonstrating more maturity and consideration. "So when did you decide to be worried by our non-return?"

"Heck, it wasn't that late. Ten thirty, eleven, maybe. I got home and Stefan was up at the house waiting for me. Said he'd called the airport when you didn't show up after dinner and heard your chopper hadn't come back."

"Wait a minute, Stefan was in the house, alone, late at night?"

"No, he was sitting on the veranda with a beer."

"I wonder— Stefan went into town early yesterday, didn't he?" The knife, the timing… A sick sensation welled in her throat. Could it have been him? But what motive would he have?

"Yeah, he went in with the first pick up of the day. Why?"

"I don't know, it's just a feeling. Look, I need to do a little work before I go to bed so I'll say goodnight."

Intelligent eyes, Phillip's eyes, pinned her, probing, prodding. "You just said you were too tired to think and now you want to do office work? Tell me why you wanted to know about Stefan." She couldn't afford to dismiss him as too young or underestimate him any longer.

"I'm trying to cover all bases. Look, I'm probably overtired and paranoid about the situation. Ignore me."

"Good evening, boss."

She jumped and put her hand over her mouth. Her manager's soft approach had caught her by surprise. "Stefan. You startled me."

"I just want to see all is good with you tonight. You okay?"

Her heart thumped and her brain was fit to explode with wild theories that she thought he'd tried to kill her, all because she'd watched him sharpen knives, which he needed to slice through pineapples. Add that to her belief Amoka had broken into her home, her concerns over the nosy journalist, and suspicions about Luc trying to seduce her to gain her plantation, and she had a grand set of worries to be going on with. If she thought much more about the string of accidents, soon she'd be able to add in Jack, the realtor, and maybe the distributor at the factory as suspects.

She was becoming paranoid.

Other than that, she was splendid. "I'm fine, thank you for your concern, Stefan, although it appears our helicopter was sabotaged. Someone seems to want me dead."

She observed him closely. His eyes widened and he shook his head in disbelief. If he was involved, he was a good actor. Or a cold-blooded killer? There was simply nothing to connect him and yet her brain stumbled and refused to let go of him as one of her suspects.

"Is not good but you here now. I patrol outside before I go to bed. Sleep well, boss. Oh, I borrow book from library last night. Was waiting long time for young boss to come home. You not mind?"

Stefan had been in the library and may well have gone into her office. Had he rifled through her papers? Or was she seeing conspiracies everywhere? *Stefan—Ivan—Russian*. She'd hidden the diary where no one would ever find it but tomorrow, she'd see about installing a safe.

"That's fine, Stefan. You're welcome to borrow books. Good night."

Stefan wandered off, soft-footed and quickly lost to view. Eva collected their empty glasses and headed to the kitchen.

Seb trailed behind. "That was weird."

"What do you mean?"

"Last night when I got home and met him on the veranda, he didn't have a book with him."

And that was more disconcerting than everything else.

***

Eva hung up the phone. Mr Willis had been more than willing to help her with her submission to the Tourism Board. Indeed, he'd been very forthcoming with information and it seemed he was on her side. Why else would he have ensured her application was couriered over to the committee meeting while she was neatly out of the way and unable to present it herself?

And if Luc was the only other major player likely to win the contract, was it possible he'd manufactured the *sabotage* of their helicopter in a bid to undermine her application? No wonder if he wanted to add their place to his. It was bigger and, with both plantations joined, he'd have been a shoe-in to win.

Unable to settle after the encounter with Stefan, she and Seb had talked long into the night about their prospects of winning the lucrative contract. Their bigger plantation versus Luc's highly efficient and well managed property.

Luc's knowledge combined with her communication skills, they'd be unbeatable. She froze, her subconscious mind screaming denial. Where had that come from? Unequivocally, it was definitely never ever going to happen. Not in a million years.

As though her brain had conjured him, he drove up the driveway and pulled up at the bottom of the steps. He strode around the Jeep, bounded up the stairs, and stood in front of her. Crinkles radiated from the corners of his eyes and shadows underlined them. He looked as though he'd slept about as well as she had, and yet he still looked good enough to eat.

"Handsome as sin and a devil to boot." The description slipped out before her tired brain could self-censor.

He removed his hat and twisted it round and round. "Devil might be a bit strong although I'm not denying I've done wrong by you. I'm here to fix that now."

"What wrong have you done me?"

"At the lagoon. It shouldn't have happened."

Was he apologizing for keeping her overnight to tip the tourism contract in his favour? Had the sabotage been no more than an elaborate pretence to keep her from submitting her proposal to the board or an attempt to seduce her into agreeing to a partnership with him? It made no more sense than her suspicions about Stefan yet without Mr Willis's generous action, she would have missed out on the opportunity to submit her proposal.

"No. It shouldn't have. There's no point to talking about it."

His gaze turned bleak, as if he was capable of feeling hurt by her words. "Fine. You don't want to talk. I get that."

His gaze slid away. Was he feeling guilty for his stunt? It

wasn't like they'd been in danger if Luc had nicked the line and yet the action didn't fit the image of the man she'd come to know. "Let's forget it. There are other—"

"So we'll find other ways of communicating. That will make for interesting evenings after we're married."

"Frankly, what you did at the lagoon was—what? What did you say?"

"Well, if you don't want to talk I know lots of mighty fine ways to pass the time."

"You're mad." Or she was. Had he really just proposed?

"I'm serious. I don't give a damn whether you want to talk or not but the fact remains, I did the wrong thing by you and I want to fix it. You could be carrying my baby."

"I—we used protection—Oh, my God, that last time—" Her hands flew to her belly. A baby. Was she even now carrying his child?

Why hadn't she thought of the possibility before? Was social ostracism as bad here as in England? With no named father and an unwed mother, what chance would the poor child have? Who was she kidding? Everyone would know Luc was the father.

"I never meant for it to happen like that. But when I'm with you, inside you—"

Hunger filled her. Deep, desperate desire for the night at the lagoon to be the truth. Their joining had been beautiful, like she'd found her missing half and she was made beautiful and completed by him. She held up a hand to stop him. "Don't, please. Spare me the romantic nonsense. It happened and the only question now is what's to be done. I may not be…pregnant…and then there's no problem."

And if she was, what then? How could she stay and care for Seb?

"Marry me. Then if we have a baby, there won't be any raised eyebrows. I can protect you."

Her entire body froze in shock. "Your choice of protection

leaves something to be desired." Bitterness tinged her tone and he winced.

"I let passion override reason but I won't let my mistake blight your life. Look, I know this isn't the way you should receive a proposal but I want to make things right for you." Somehow he had manoeuvred her back to a chair. He took both her hands in his and sat her down. She sat willingly, unreality having unbalanced her usually even keel.

Luc went down on one knee. "Eva, marry me?"

Chapter Fifteen

Eva stood at the back of the Planters' Club and tapped her foot in time with the music. The local jazz band was good and the current song, *Perfidia*, suited her mood as she watched the swirl of passing dancers. Subconsciously, she rubbed the single emerald of her necklace between her fingers. Every introduction this evening had been accompanied by covert or less subtle glances at the stone and she could almost hear their thoughts—heiress—as she smiled and exchanged pleasantries.

She finished her soda and scanned the crowded floor. Designer dresses sparkled among a sea of black and white dinner jackets. Not one of the men looked as good as Luc, in or out of his tuxedo. Which thought was of little consequence. She spotted him, hand in pocket and deep in conversation with an older gentleman at the bar. Handsome as sin she'd thought him. But his good looks and dancing skills were irrelevant. They were here for one purpose only. If she was pregnant, their little charade would set up their *relationship* in the eyes of the local community and give their quick marriage credibility.

Marriage. To Luc.

Scarcely able to believe she'd agreed to his proposal, she dreaded hearing it made public. He'd wanted to announce it this evening but she'd put her foot down. "It would be as good as saying we did the deed while we were stranded. Please say nothing."

Reluctantly he'd agreed but even one-eyed Freddie could read his silent statement. He and Eva Abbott were an item. Would-be dance partners were deterred by his hand on her back, by the possessive tone when he introduced her. By the way he invaded her personal space and she said nothing. By now, there could be little doubt in anyone's mind.

But if she wasn't pregnant—

She simply didn't know what she wanted where Luc Martineau was concerned. Other than this burning desire for things to be different. To be real.

A ripple of awareness ran through the crowd and heads turned, drawing her distracted attention to a stunning couple near the bar. Luc seemed to be wearing a gorgeous brunette in a white sheath dress shimmering with white sequins. Olive-skinned—an almost indecent amount of bare back was revealed between glittering spaghetti straps—the brunette had her arms draped around Luc's neck. And Luc's hands were on her waist.

The desire to scratch out the eyes of the woman plastered to Luc's chest was sharp and unexpected. To pluck her red-painted talons from his neck and step in between them while casually demanding she unhand her fiancé.

Good grief, she would sound like a jealous lover.

Heat and the press of many bodies in close confinement became claustrophobic as she battled the crazy green-eyed monster leering at her. If Luc meant nothing to her, why was she jealous?

Several heads turned in her direction and she caught a name—Genevieve Benson—murmured over and over.

Eva licked her lips and set her empty glass on a nearby table. Her head ached from two glasses of champagne and a sudden need for solitude. Tired of waiting for Luc to return and tired of pretending to enjoy herself while the woman who'd dumped him made like a rash, she straightened her spine and glided from the room. He could come looking for her. Or not. She'd show him she couldn't care less what he did.

She slipped through the throng on the veranda. People congregated in small groups and couples, but at least out here the breeze was pleasant and the lights low. She nodded to a few acquaintances but kept moving until she reached the quietest, darkest spot. Tucked behind a huge potted palm, she leaned on the railing, lifted the weight of hair off her neck, and breathed deeply.

Cigar smoke drifted on the night air, Cuban and expensive. It was followed by men's voices.

"Looks like the Tourism Board is going to overlook Martineau in favour of that little redhead who bought Benson's place. Bigger spread, more potential, especially with a looker like her as a draw card. Imagine coming home to her every evening."

She froze. They were talking about her. Luc and her and the contract.

"With Benson on the Board, would you expect a different outcome? It wouldn't have mattered if the only other contender was Mickey Mouse. Benson would never let a Martineau succeed after Gloria married Henri instead of him."

"He's still pissed that Martineau proposed to his daughter."

"Not to worry. Martineau will get hold of it one way or another. D'ya see he's brought the redhead tonight. Won't let anyone else near her. Bet he's already staked his claim, if you know what I mean."

The other man sniggered. "Wouldn't mind tumbling her myself."

"You wouldn't have a hope. Martineau can't keep his eyes off her."

"Or his hands. You know what the emergency was? He wanted to get—" The men moved back around the corner and their voices were lost in the general hubbub.

Her stomach heaved. She'd seen the dirty winks and heard the sly nudges in the men's tones. If these men were talking about her like that now, how much worse would it be if she bore Luc's child out of wedlock? If only she knew if she was pregnant. She breathed through her mouth and swallowed. She absolutely could not, would not be sick here.

Luc would do anything to get his hands on Benson's property. Wasn't that what Jack had told her?

Did that include deliberately making her pregnant so they

would have to marry? Did he believe he could get his hands on her property that way?

Her stomach churned as pieces fell into place. Would Luc really stoop so low? Had she given him a way to steal her land by falling for his charms, his sympathy? She slapped her hands over her mouth to quell the rising nausea and her fears.

Luc returned to the spot where he'd last seen Eva. He hadn't intended to get caught up in a discussion on the state of the export market but without being rude, he'd had to stay when old Heck badgered him for his opinion. Several men had been eying Eva all evening and chances were one of them had convinced her to take to the floor. He scanned the dancers but her distinctive auburn curls tumbling down her back and her delicious curves were missing in action. Was it possible she'd seen Genevieve throw herself into his arms like long-lost family and misinterpreted the scene? No, Eva would have to care about him to be jealous.

He'd stayed firmly by her side and for most of the evening they'd circulated and chatted with other planters. Lord knew he was having enough trouble controlling his desire for her without holding her close in front of so many witnesses. One duty dance with Eva had nearly killed him while Genevieve had pinned her body to his and he'd felt nothing. Not true. He was annoyed.

Mitzy Stark appeared in front of him and tapped his arm with her fan. "Hi, hon, misplaced that gorgeous girl you came in with?"

"Yes, have you seen Eva?"

"Sure did. She was on her way out to the car park. Looked a little peaky if you ask me. Anything I can do?"

Why was Eva out in the car park? And unwell? Was this one of those signs of pregnancy? He couldn't very well ask Mitzy. It would be all over the island before he reached his car. *Think.* "Thanks, Mitzy, no. Eva mentioned having a headache earlier. She was in the fields today and forgot her hat. I expect she's gone out for some air."

"Silly girl. With that fair complexion and red hair, she should always wear a hat."

"True. I'll find her and see if she wants to go home. Goodnight."

It took him several minutes to escape the round of goodbyes and reach his car. If Eva had been headed in this direction, he'd missed her. He circled back through the garden, disturbing a couple in a dark bower but coming up empty-handed. Where was she?

Preoccupied, he returned to his Jeep. Had she found a ride home with someone else? But why, without telling him?

Heck Adams was smoking a cigarillo beside his car and ambled over. "Not allowed to smoke these beauties anymore. Doctor's orders. Don't tell my wife, eh, Luc, my boy?" He dragged in a lungful and held it for a while before exhaling, then tapped him on the arm with the hand holding the cigarillo. Ash flecked his sleeve as the glowing tip of the cigarillo wove a lazy path back up to Heck's mouth. "Just wanted to say it's a damned disgrace the way Benson's manipulating the Board."

His mind wasn't on Heck Adams and his foul-smelling cigarillos or Benson and the board for that matter. Eva's auburn curls and green eyes filled his thoughts as he ran a hand through his hair and searched for a polite response. "What are you talking about?"

"The Tourism Board contract. They're talking about awarding it to your little redhead. Damned stupid move, and I told 'em so. Need someone with experience and a stake in the island, not an English accent and a pretty face."

Great way to cap a shitty evening. Lost: one fiancée and one tourism contract. Could he make it three strikes?

"She looked pasty when she asked Jack Lyons for a ride home."

Strike three.

"Jack took Eva home?"

"Guess she couldn't find you. Word to the wise, my boy, awfully poor form to let another man take your woman home. She might think you don't love her. Night." He shoved the cigarillo between his teeth and strolled away.

He watched Heck's receding back and wondered what the hell he was doing standing alone in a car park when Jack was probably even now escorting Eva up her front stairs. He ground his teeth and thumped the panel of his Jeep.

Eva and Jack—alone. Not going to happen.

He swung into the driver's seat and floored the Jeep out of the car park and along the dark road leading to Eva's place. Why had she left without him? Why did she ask Jack for a lift?

Jack seemed content to drive at a leisurely speed when all Eva wanted was to get home and sleep. Her head thumped and her heart ached while her stomach felt like she'd just disembarked from a rollercoaster ride. No matter how she felt about Luc, it was clear he didn't reciprocate. Genevieve Benson seemed to be very much on his mind. And after his body.

"We might have missed out on a dance tonight but driving you home is reward for my patience." Jack leaned an elbow through his open window and tossed a predatory grin her way. Was he flirting with her? How had she missed that before?

"Reward? I'm sorry but I don't understand your meaning, Mr Lyons."

"Jack, please. I thought you might want to talk to me about the letter I sent you."

"I haven't received a letter from you. What's it about?"

"I did some ferreting around about your family's previous connection with the Islands and found the property they bought. I included a map showing its position. Would you like me to take you there?"

She frowned and dragged her wayward attention back to

Jack. "You mean it's here, on Oahu?"

Jack grinned and nodded. "Not far from here in fact. It's been abandoned for a number of years but yes, it exists."

Maybe Luc had been right all along. His pirate playground fit Jack's description. "Why did you search for a property we haven't owned in more than a century?"

"An heiress might want to buy back the land her family owned. Who knows what treasures you might discover along the way? And you might be nice to the man who helped you reconnect with your history."

Heiress. That wretched newspaper story seemed determined to undermine her efforts at creating a new life for Seb and her. Did everyone think they had money to burn? She bit back a sarcastic comment and laughed inwardly at the irony. Heiresses didn't dirty their nails working on their plantations.

But heiresses do get targeted by people out to skim money from them. And if there were others besides Jack who thought she had hidden money or an emerald necklace, like that stupid article had implied, she and Seb might be in danger.

She looked across at Jack. Several times he'd referred to her as the heiress. Was it possible he really believed that story? She rubbed the emerald between finger and thumb. If it came from the original necklace, maybe it carried a curse. For certain it hadn't brought her any joy.

He reached for a packet of cigarettes on the dashboard and tapped one out, offering the pack to her. "Want one?"

She shook her head. "No, thanks."

Jack tucked the cigarette in the corner of his mouth and raised a fancy silver lighter to the tip. A tiny flame illuminated his features, creating odd shadows as he drew in a lungful of smoke. With a flick, he closed the lighter but a ghost-light continued to dance in her vision. Was she seeing enemies where none existed or did Jack hunger for the untold wealth of the emerald necklace as well?

###

Luc was close to Eva's plantation when a car turned out of her driveway onto the main road and headed towards him. Even at night, Jack's sedan was distinctive with its colourful paint job. He grinned in the darkness. Jack would be pissed off at not being invited to stay for coffee.

He pulled over and waited for Jack to do the same. "Is Eva okay?"

"I wouldn't say okay. Said she's got a headache or whatever women have when they don't want us around. You're not welcome. What did you do, aside from disappear on her?"

"Long story. Later." He waved a half-salute at his friend and drove the few hundred yards to her house.

Lights showed through the bay window of her office and the fan light above the front door. He mounted the stairs, knocked and waited. A curtain twitched in the reception room and a band of light flicked across his face then the light was switched off.

He waited.

A floorboard creaked on the other side of the door followed by a soft sniffle and a hiccough. He put his ear to the wood and listened. What in God's name was going on? Worry kicked up another notch and his chest tightened. Had she discovered she was pregnant? How long did it take to know for sure?

"Eva? I know you're there. Open the door and talk to me." The door remained closed.

He pounded with his fist on the panel. "Eva, so help me I'll break down this goddamn door if you won't talk to me. What's wrong?"

"Go away. We've nothing to say to one another." Tremulous, her voice on the other side of the wood sounded so un-Eva-like it scared him. Was she crying? What had happened to the passionate woman who made every day worth living for the chance of seeing her? He was losing her. After their day and night at the lagoon, he couldn't lose her because she'd become too important to him, because he wanted to have that chance with her—because—because—

Crap, Heck recognized it before he had.

He loved Eva.

Stunned by the realization, he rested his forehead against the door. Heart thumping as though it would explode, he dragged air into his lungs. Love? Not possible. Love made people vulnerable, opened them up to hurt. Like his father.

Seconds ticked past as Luc's memories of his father blurred, shifted and refocused with startling clarity.

Like his father who was now blissfully happy with Jayne.

He pushed upright and stared at the wooden door. On the other side was Eva, who didn't want to see him or talk to him. Whose biggest fears revolved around protecting her nephew's inheritance and the possibility of social ostracism as an unwed mother if he couldn't convince her to marry him.

Failure was not an option. He would be like his father, strong enough to try again.

"Eva? Listen to me. I don't care about the contract, or buying this place. All I want is to marry you."

A sob, quickly muffled, reached him and a sliding sound. He pressed his palms and ear to the door. Eva was there, upset, maybe ill. Because of him. Because she was carrying his child? Now was not the time for declarations of love and promises of forever.

He moved swiftly around the side of the house. A curtain fluttered in the gentle breeze at one of the library windows. He opened it wider, gripped the sides, and pulled himself inside. The room was in darkness, bar a sliver of light through the almost closed doorway. He felt his way across the floor, swearing when he cracked his shin on the corner of a piece of furniture. He reached the door and stepped into the hallway. A sigh of relief was immediately replaced by a lump of cold, hard dread sinking like lead in the pit of his stomach.

Eva slumped in a froth of white and silver at the front door. Head on her knees and arms wrapped around her legs, she had never looked more vulnerable. Had he brought her to this? Bile rose in his throat, even as he kneeled beside her. He wanted to fold her into his arms and never let her go but his wants were not what mattered now. He had to make things right for her, even if it meant convincing her to take his name and never touching her again. Whatever she wanted, even *that* he would do for her. Just let her be okay.

"Eva?"

She stiffened at the sound of his voice but didn't look at him. "Go away."

"Not until I know you're okay."

"I'm fine."

"I hate to disagree but obviously, you're not. Why did you run away from the dance?"

"I had a headache."

"Why didn't you tell me? I would have driven you home."

"I might have but three's a crowd and I do hate a crush." Bracing herself against the door she rose unsteadily to her feet and smoothed her skirt with a hand that trembled a little.

"I don't understand. What threesome do you mean?"

"Don't you think it excessive to have sex with one woman and ask her to marry you when you've already got a—mistress shall we call her—on the side?"

"Mistress?"

"The woman attached to your chest at the bar."

Genevieve.

With a bottle or more of champagne under her belt, she'd staggered into his arms and clung. Three sheets to the wind, her partner had laughed and dropped into a nearby chair while Luc tried to detach her from his neck.

"That was Genevieve Benson."

Eva's lips parted and her eyes widened. "Gen—the woman

153

you were going to marry? Well, isn't that cosy? But I don't share, Luc."

"Good to know because I don't share either. Don't ever ask Jack Lyons or any other man apart from Seb to drive you home again."

She grabbed the door handle in a white-knuckled grip. Like a magnificent flaming-haired goddess, she drew herself up to her full height and glared at him. "Don't expect me to put up with your floozy flaunting herself all—"

"You're jealous. My God, there's hope for us yet if a drunk woman falling into my arms makes you green-eyed."

"I'm not jealous. I'd have to care about you for that to happen but I will not be made a fool of. You wanted this marriage—"

"I get it. But asking Jack to drive you home only fuels suspicion and gossip. Do you really want that?"

"Don't be absurd. Of course not. But if you want us to marry, I need to know I can trust you on something as basic as fidelity. No more Genevieves, drunk or otherwise."

God, he knew all about abused trust. So how could he expect Eva to trust him when he'd shown her she couldn't? Somehow he had to earn her trust.

"Agreed, and no more Jacks. It works both ways." He took a deep breath and brushed his fingers down her cheek. "I never meant to hurt you. Marry me and put the rumour and innuendo to rest. It's a small world on the island and people have long memories."

He stood, holding his breath. A chance, that's all he asked. Would she give him one more chance?

Chapter Sixteen

Gritty-eyed from lack of sleep and overdosed on emotional turmoil, Eva stood under the shower. Overhearing the planters' conversation last night had been a rude awakening. As had seeing the Benson woman draped around Luc like a vine. Jealousy surged again. Until that moment she'd deluded herself that perhaps she and Luc could make a go of it. Sexual compatibility wasn't common, if the whispers she'd heard were true. At least in that area they were on the same page. But what about out of bed? What if there was no trust? Or love?

That embrace at the bar had shaken her trust in Luc's offer. It had been an accident, she understood that now but it had exposed her deepest fear. Did she trust Luc? Deep down, she still couldn't reconcile the idea he wanted her more than her plantation. Was she giving more weight to Jack's description of Luc than to Luc's actions? There were times, many if she was honest, when Luc had been kind and generous. And sexy. She thumped the shower screen and turned off the water.

Preoccupied with her anxiety, she hadn't looked for Jack's letter nor thought to look in on Seb. He'd probably already left for work. She brushed her teeth, her hair, and swallowed a couple of headache tablets. Defiantly, she tugged her hair back into a high pony tail, pulled on shorts and a blouse and headed down the hallway.

Several letters lay on the silver salver on the hall table. She flicked through them but Jack's letter wasn't among them. Perhaps it would arrive in today's delivery. Carrying the rest of the mail, Eva pushed open the office door and froze. Papers lay strewn across the floor as though a tornado had hit. Drawers lay in tumbled chaos. She stepped gingerly through the mess to the desk, trying not to move anything. Had the burglar found what she feared he was looking for?

Only Seb and she knew the desk had secret compartments. If it was gone— Hands shaking, she depressed a piece of ornate carving and the secret drawer sprang open.

Empty. Oh, God, where was Seb? What if he'd been here and tried to stop the intruder?

"Seb!" She raced into his bedroom and her heart sank. The bed was made and the room tidy, just as she'd left it the morning before. Yesterday's work clothes were missing from his clothes hamper. Had he even made it home from work?

She searched his bedside table and dresser, looking for a note, a clue, anything to tell her he was safe. If he hadn't made it home, then what?

Maybe he'd spent the night with the boys. If they played poker he might have slept in the bunkhouse, knowing she would be late in from the ball. First she needed to phone Luc and find out if Seb was there. Then—but what if he wasn't at Luc's? What if something had happened to him?

She pushed away from the desk and ran out of the house. Yesterday, Stefan had mentioned maintenance issues he needed to work on. She prayed he was still working in the shed and not out in the fields. But when she flung open the door to the machinery shed, it was empty. No Stefan, no motorbike, and her car was missing. She frowned, trying to remember if Stefan had asked to borrow it, or if she'd heard the engine this morning.

Shaking her head, she dashed back to the office and phoned Luc's place.

Samuel answered. "Haven't seen Seb since he left here early evening to go home. Everything okay, Miss Abbott?"

Her heart sank along with her hopes that he was safely at work. "Not really. Please have him call me if he turns up. Thanks, Samuel."

She dropped her head onto her hands. What had she brought Seb into? If they had stayed in England, he would have been safe. "Why didn't Luc come to the phone, Samuel?"

"He's outside checking for footprints. We had a break-in last night and someone went through his office."

"*You* had a break in, too?" What the heck was going on? And why did the news make her feel better?

"We called the police but they expect to be a while. You want I should send them over to you to talk about Seb, Miss?"

"Yes, please, thanks." She hung up. There was so much more going on than she could have imagined. Why had Luc been targeted? Because somebody thought they were a couple? That she had told him about—what? The diary, the necklace? Methodically, she searched the shelves in the library. Deep within, she knew it was pointless. Both Seb and the diary were gone.

Nerves fragile and brain reeling, she went to the library and poured a finger of brandy. She swallowed a mouthful and coughed, her eyes watering and her throat burning. Unsure what to do next, she carried the glass out to the veranda and leaned against a post.

"Bit early in the day to hit the bottle, isn't it?" Luc climbed the side steps, stopped in front of her and shoved his hands in his pockets. Stubble shadowed his jaw, as dark as his eyes.

"Samuel said Seb is missing. I'm here to help you find him." His gaze held hers and she had the impression he could see deep inside her soul. He knew her, inside and out, every damaged part of her and he still wanted her.

She nodded. "Thank you. And—can we talk about—us— after we work out where Seb is?"

Luc shrugged but a flash of something like hope sparked through him. Wanting to talk about *them* felt like a step forward from cautious Eva. He looked at the flat plane of her stomach. "Do you want to sit down? Is your headache gone? How are you this morning?"

She gave him an odd look and he realized he was intruding in her personal space again.

He needed to keep a lid on it, at least until they had worked out where Seb was. Huge green eyes looked up at him. Primal man lurked just below his civilized veneer, ready to throw her over his shoulder and take her home and keep her safe. Acting like a cave man held a certain attraction, and not only if her life was at risk.

She touched his arm again and his restraint cracked. He wrapped his arms about her. It felt so right holding her. Why couldn't she see this was where she belonged? In his arms and in his heart. His father was right. Whatever it took, he would risk it all for a chance with Eva.

The sweet scent of Eva filled his nose, roses and lilies and her unique smell. Softly, he stroked a hand over her back, massaged her neck and pressed a kiss to her forehead. And it dawned on him she'd pulled her hair up into a tie, revealing the long, elegant arch of her neck. The top of her scar was barely visible above her blouse. A small variation for most women, the change of hairstyle was huge for Eva. She'd paid attention to his suggestion. The thought pleased him and added to his optimistic outlook. Maybe they would work out after all.

She pressed her head into his shoulder. They stood for a moment, wrapped in their own thoughts until she stepped back and he released his hold. "What should we do first? Ring the police?"

"I doubt they'll list Seb as missing until he's been gone more than twenty-four hours. He could still turn up. Although if he went out last night, it wasn't with any of my boys."

"You asked them?"

"Samuel checked after your call. Acky and Moe are worried. When they asked him to stay for another poker party Seb told them he had to head home. Moe thought Seb had something on his mind but didn't share what it was."

"There's more."

"Tell me what you know."

"Follow me."

She opened the door into her office and stood aside to

allow him access. He stepped into a snowdrift of paper covering the floor. Her desk was a lone island in the middle of a sea of paper, with one small, clear patch in the centre.

He grabbed her shoulder and turned her to look at him. "When did you discover this? Was it like this when you came in last night?" Her eyes widened and he tamped down the fear that surged through him at the thought of her alone in the house with an intruder. He relaxed his hold and tried to contain his need to shield her from every bad thing. She didn't need him losing his cool, too.

"I have no idea. I wasn't exactly in the mood to do office work when I got home. I took a tablet for my headache and went straight to bed."

Two things registered at the same time—Mitzy Stark had been right about Eva looking unwell, and Eva hadn't been aware of the invasion of her home. Concern and relief warred within him.

"I'm okay aside from not knowing where Seb is. His motorbike is missing—my car, too—but it doesn't look like he's been home. Samuel said your place was broken into, too?"

"While we were at the ball. I discovered the break-in when I got home."

"Then they were most likely going through my office while we were out. I think whoever did it was long gone by the time we came home."

"Of course they knew we'd be at the ball together. Every planter on the island was probably there last night." But had they counted on Seb's presence or had he caught them in the act? A frisson of worry at Seb's continued absence niggled at him.

Eva touched his arm and frowned. "But why would they hit your place? Was anything taken?"

He sat on the corner of her desk and folded his arms. "I have a theory. Maybe when the thieves couldn't find what they wanted here they decided you'd given it to me for safekeeping. They tried to break into my safe."

Her stricken gaze tugged at him. "I'm sorry for dragging

you into this. If we weren't putting on an appearance of being—of us going out together, you might not have been burgled."

"Can't you even say it? Of us being a couple. Christ, I'm sorry things happened the way they did. I wish I'd courted you properly so you'd believe I want to marry you for who you are. *You*, Eva. Not because I want your land or because I've tarnished your reputation in the eyes of society." He paced to the window and raked a hand through his hair.

The focus had to stay on Seb and how to find him.

His gaze ran over the paper on the floor. What had caught his eye? A pattern? "I think it was the same guy or guys. The method of searching is the same."

Eva spread her arms wide, bemused as she indicated her office floor. "How can you tell anything from this mess?"

"There's something we're not seeing. Show me how you'd search the desk."

Eva looked thoughtful then picked up a pretend piece of paper, examined it, and tossed it on the floor beside her.

"You toss it to the right because you're right-handed."

Eva looked at the floor to her right then examined the other side. "Most of the mess is on the left. Do you think the intruder was a left-hander?"

"I'm no expert but it makes sense. Did Seb come home last night?"

"He may have. Samuel said he left your place early in the evening but his bed wasn't slept in and it doesn't look like he had dinner. The kitchen's clean. I'm worried he may have surprised the intruder."

Eva shook her head. "This place should be called the Bermuda Triangle. Seb is missing, his bike is gone, so is my car, my manager hasn't checked in. I should never have brought Seb here. Promise you won't disappear too, Luc?"

He cupped her cheek and met her green gaze. "I'll stick around as long as you need me. I'm still hoping you'll consider the forever option."

The phone rang, the sound jarring in the charged silence.

Eva blinked and reached for the receiver. "Hello, Seb… Who is this?" She straightened and blanched.

He tensed, every muscle ready for action. Her face told the tale and it wasn't good news.

"I understand. Yes, alone." She hung up blindly and sank into the chair. Shoulders stiff, she sat for several heartbeats. "Oh, God, Luc, Seb's been kidnapped."

Chapter Seventeen

"Tell me exactly what they said." Threaded with steel, Luc's voice anchored Eva in a world gone mad. He hunkered down in front of her and his hands enclosed hers, warm and strong, and holding her to him when she felt in danger of disappearing down some malevolent black hole. Like Seb.

She would not put his life at risk, too. It had to do be done by her alone.

Eva shook her head. "I can't tell anyone. If I do, they'll kill him."

His eyes narrowed, and he pinned her with his intent gaze. His hold on her hands tightened. "Don't think I'm going to let you go into danger. It's not going to happen."

"Seb is my nephew and my responsibility. I have to protect him."

"You're his guardian and you're like a lioness defending her cub but you are not doing it alone. Not now."

Her heart wanted to sing at his words, at the promise he would be by her side now and—later. But she couldn't let him. Not if she was to get Seb back alive.

"I have to go. I'll take my father's gun."

"You're not Annie Oakley. I didn't teach you to shoot so you could go looking for bad guys. I can do whatever they asked of you."

He was offering to go in her place? To put himself in danger for Seb and her? Why? A lump formed in her throat. Her brother had been the last man protective of her. Like Phil, Luc was prepared to put himself in the firing line. For her. She swallowed the desire to burst into tears. Kind as his offer was, the responsibility was hers.

"I don't doubt you'd try, but if I don't do exactly what they told me, Seb will pay the price. I can't risk his life. This is something I have to do by myself."

Her heart pounded as she pulled her hands out of his hold and stood. Time was running out and Luc could be too persuasive. If he continued urging her to let him go in her place, she might be tempted to give in. Where was that blasted stiff British upper lip when she needed it? She sniffed, straightened her shoulders, and turned to leave. She got no further than a pace toward the door before his arms wrapped around her. Locked in his embrace, she looked up into the stormiest pair of dark eyes she'd ever seen. Hypnotic and compelling, his gaze pinned her as surely as his arms.

"Okay, here's the deal. You tell me what they want and we'll make a plan together. If need be, you make a solo appearance but I *will* be nearby and I'll have the gun."

"But—"

"This is non-negotiable. I am not letting you walk into God knows what danger without being by your side. Or as close as I can without putting Seb at greater risk. Now, tell me, what did they say?"

A burden shared. She exhaled and bit down on her lip. Making up her mind suddenly seemed easy.

"There's a cottage up in the hills. From the highway near the airfield, I have to take the dirt road on the right and follow it for about two miles until I reach a blue mail box. There will be further instructions inside. No police, and no one else is to know."

He nodded. "I know the place. It's an old farmhouse. Not suitable for long-term habitation but close to the airfield. They must figure you'll give them what they want and they'll make a quick getaway by air."

"Sounds likely. But I can't give them what they want."

"What are they demanding?"

The impossible. "Josephine's emerald necklace. I don't

even know if it still exists as a single piece of jewellery, but I don't have it to exchange for Seb." And that fact made it so much more dangerous for Seb. She wished she'd never read Josephine's diary, never mentioned it to Seb and gotten his hopes up about hunting for treasure. "Seb probably talked about it as though he knew where it was. Whoever's taken him thinks we have it or know where it is. I have to rescue him."

"What are you planning to do? Walk up to the kidnappers' front door and say 'here I am, take me instead'?"

She sucked in a breath. What was she going to do? Without the necklace, she had nothing to bargain with. Except herself. "I'll do whatever it takes to save Seb."

"Let me think." He released her, paced to the window and stood, rubbing his chin as he looked out.

Without the necklace, she could see no alternative. The plantation wasn't worth enough to offer in exchange. Empty-handed, she doubted she would be allowed close to the cottage to even attempt the negotiation. Maybe if she took a white flag they'd talk to her?

Luc strode across the rug and planted his fists on her desk, startling her. "You said they demanded the necklace so we need something to make them think we have it. What about we dummy up a box big enough to hold it?"

"Why? I don't have it."

"But they'll think you do. The boys and I will surround the place and then you approach the mailbox holding a box in your hands. For sure they'll have you under surveillance and people see what they want to. It might be enough to get to the next stage of negotiations."

"I'll do it. How big a box do you think we need?"

He shook his head. "Eva, you have the strangest grasp of danger at times. Okay, you find a box and fill it with something. What about putting in that emerald you wore last night? If the worst happens and the kidnappers open the box before we reach them, they might believe it's a sign of good faith on your part."

Eva nodded. "What if I add a key? One that looks like it belongs to a safety deposit box?"

"Good idea. It might buy us more time to rescue Seb. Wrap the package well. I'll alert the police and the authorities at the airfield in case the kidnappers slip through our fingers. Samuel will arm the boys who can handle a gun." He cupped her face and looked into her eyes. "We will rescue Seb, and we'll bring him home.

Eva took one hand off the wheel and wiped her palm down her skirt. Luc's Jeep bounced into a rut in the dirt track, the steering wheel jibbed, and her sunglasses slipped down her nose. She grabbed the wheel with both hands and hoped like crazy they'd be in time to meet the kidnapper's demands.

"Breathe, Eva. I'll tell you when to stop so I can get out before we're in sight of the cottage. Trust me."

Luc's presence calmed her. She was sure that was why he'd insisted on accompanying her rather than going in with his men but the closer they got to the kidnappers, the more her anxiety grew. She'd be a basket case by now without Luc beside her.

He had organized his men to be in place and she was ready to go in just on sunset. "You'll be a more difficult target with the sun behind you."

"Great, thanks for that." Thinking of herself as a target sent shivers down her spine but it was no use getting cold feet now. Seb needed her.

"If I could convince you not to put yourself in the firing line, I would. Short of tying you up, which I'm sorely tempted to do, the next best thing is to reduce your exposure as much as possible."

She risked a glance at his profile and quickly looked back at the rough track. "What is it with you and tying people up, Luc?"

He chuckled and leaned over to brush a strand of hair

behind her ear. "Not *people*, Eva. You. Just you."

"Bound and helpless?"

"Safe and away from here."

Luc scanned the vegetation on her side of the road, touched her arm and pointed to a bend up ahead. "Pull over just before we reach the bend. I'll get out there."

"Are we there already?" She stopped the car and pulled on the hand brake. She could do this. She could march up to the cottage and be part of rescuing Seb. Luc gave her the courage to do it and much more; he made her strong. Her heart swelled with the knowledge and she knew she had to tell him now, before it was too late, in case something happened.

"Luc, before you go, I want to tell you—"

He touched a finger to her lips. "Why don't you tell me tonight, when we're home again?"

"But—"

"Sssh. Give me five minutes to get in place then drive up to the mailbox. Do it exactly like they said and make sure you keep that jewellery box in plain sight. And Eva, under no circumstances are you to enter that cottage. Got it?"

She nodded. "Got it. And Luc, thank you."

He jumped out of the car and reached into the back for his rifle and a box of ammunition. He slung the rifle over his shoulder, rounded the car, and stopped beside her window.

She looked into his strong face. Would they rescue Seb? Would they both be alive to ask and answer that question tonight? Her heart beat hard while his eyes locked with hers. Dark and compelling, they communicated his absolute belief in her and in them. She swallowed the doubts and fears pounding in her brain and forced tight muscles into a little smile.

"No promises, but one. I'll move heaven and earth to keep you and Seb safe. After that—"

"One step at a time. Be careful." If only she could wrap Luc in her arms and keep him safe. If only she'd kept Seb safe. She gripped the wheel harder until not only her knuckles, but both hands paled.

"That's enough for now. Remember, no matter what, do not go inside. Stay safe." He slipped into the bushes and was immediately lost to sight.

She strained to hear his passage through the thick vegetation. Late afternoon breeze rustled the leaves and covered any sound but it whispered his last words like a prayer. *Stay safe.*

Seconds crawled past. A lifetime. She gave herself license to remember another lifetime before knowledge of such evil as she now faced had tainted her life. When her worst fear was failing Chemistry. Phillip had tutored her.

I'm so sorry, Phillip. I promised to look after Seb for you. If Luc rescues him—when Luc rescues him—I'm going to try to do what you would have wanted for him. I'll give him space to spread his wings and fly. But if you're up there looking down, please, help us.

She turned the key in the ignition and eased onto the track. It couldn't be much farther. She searched the bushes on her side of the road in the direction Luc had taken, both hoping and fearing to see him. There was nothing, no flash of movement or glint off a weapon. Had she really expected to see anything?

She crested a rise and the cottage came into view, nestled in the middle of a small, cleared block. And there, beside a low, straggly bush, was the mailbox.

She hit the brakes and Luc's Jeep stalled. Her chest hit the steering wheel, smacking the breath out of her. She jerked the hand brake on and fisted both hands in her lap. In the peaceful afternoon, her breathing sounded harsh and loud. Darting sideways glances from behind the screen of her sunglasses, she faced the cottage.

What was it Phillip used to say? *Face down your enemy. It takes away some of their power. Stay cool and calm on the outside, even if inside you're a seething mess of fear.*

She picked up the dummy package and opened the door, smoothed her skirt down and lifted her chin.

The distance to the mailbox was a mere five yards of dirt and stones but it felt more like five miles. She clutched the package in front of her and walked slowly towards it. Faded letters on the side proclaimed she was standing in front of Swenson's Farm. The post leaned at a drunken angle and the catch was stiff with rust. It refused to open to her fumbling, one-handed attempts.

She placed the package at her feet, then, two-handed, she grasped the flap, tugged and was rewarded with a loud, metallic grating sound followed by the flap opening half way. And there it stayed, refusing to budge further.

Gingerly, she reached into the mailbox and withdrew a folded slip of paper. An elegant, capital A was embossed in the centre top of the page. Her personal stationery. Was this to make sure she knew they'd been in her house, that they weren't bluffing?

She turned her attention to the three lines of scrawled instructions. Twice she read it through then looked up the sloping garden to the cottage.

Blank, dirty windows remained empty. Somehow, she'd expected to see them watching from the cottage.

Aware that Luc was watching her every reaction, she clenched her teeth and locked her knees. He must not guess her intentions before she reached her goal or he would try to stop her. And if he did, Seb would die.

She picked up the fake package and weighed it in her hands. Was it realistic enough to convince the kidnappers and give her a chance to get Seb out of there? She pressed her lips together and sent up a prayer.

Luc would have a fit if he knew what she planned. It had taken several changes of clothes to find a full skirt with a belt to help hold the weight and a deep enough pocket to hide her father's service revolver. Every exposed step of the walk from the mailbox to the cottage, she was conscious of the weight of the box and the hidden gun banging against her thigh.

As she approached the front door, the setting sun reflected off the windows in blinding golden starbursts. She blinked and tried to focus on the ground ahead. Her cockeyed plan needed two clear eyes and a truckload of good luck to succeed.

She stopped ten feet from the door, lowered the package to the ground and backed a couple of steps away, palms open and hands spread wide. Her heart raced as adrenaline coursed through her body.

The door cracked open and the tip of a rifle poked through.

A bead of sweat ran down Luc's neck as he lined up his shot. Eva was completely exposed in that wasteland of a garden. Every step she took towards the door added more grey hairs to his head. In vain he'd argued all afternoon to take her place and make the delivery but she refused to be swayed.

"Seb's my responsibility. I have to be the one. Don't you think the kidnappers will suspect something is fishy if you show up in my place?"

Of course she was right, but it didn't make the waiting any easier. Halfway up the garden slope and she was still moving. "Far enough, Eva," he muttered. "That's enough. Why aren't you stopping?"

"Hey, boss, the boys are in position. The place is surrounded. How many guns you see?" Samuel eased into full length commando position on Luc's right and sighted along the barrel of his rifle.

Luc flicked a glance at him, checked the boys on his left, and focused back on the door. He needed Eva to stop short of the house so he had a clear shot. *If* they came out. "One at the door and another at the left hand window. I'll take the door. Did you see any more from the side?" Luc flexed his trigger hand and resumed his grip. He sighted the gun at the window then trained it to cover the door. The man and the gun directly threatening Eva.

"Couldn't spot any other guns but the boys have the back covered. Miss Abbott's car and Seb's bike are in the shed. Wish we knew how many are in there and if they've got more guns."

"At least two. One to drive the car and another, the bike. They probably took the bike to make Eva think Seb was out and buy themselves more time."

"Pretty weird, eh, boss? Any ideas who took Seb?"

"My money's on the Russian. He hasn't been seen since yesterday. His accomplice is anyone's guess."

"Piece of shit, no-good bastard. I'd like to wring his neck for what he's doing to poor Miss Abbott and Seb."

"Get in line, Samuel. I've got first dibs on him." And he planned to see the bastard went to jail and the key was thrown away.

Out of the corner of his eye, Luc saw Samuel grin. "Thought so."

"Don't look so smug, Samuel. I'm marrying that woman, come hell or high water."

"'Bout time, boss."

Luc grunted at Samuel and held his breath until Eva stopped about ten feet from the door. Slowly, she placed the box on the ground and stepped back a couple of paces. "Atta girl, keep going. Get out of there—"

He wished there'd been some way to know what the note had directed her to do. The suspense was killing him. She stopped again, palms spread to show she was unarmed. What did they expect, for Chrissakes? That she'd go in guns blazing?

"Boss, there's someone at the other window. That's three."

"She's not moving. Get out of there, Eva. Come on, baby, leave now." Adrenaline surged through him. Watching the woman he loved walking into the devil's lair was wrong on every level. His muscles wanted to propel him down there and put his body between her and the line of fire. Against his screaming instinct, he pressed into the earth. She wouldn't thank him for putting her life above Seb's.

Light glinted off the barrel of the gun in the doorway as the shooter signalled Eva to come forward. Luc's heart pounded and he swallowed the shout clawing to escape him. "No. Don't go inside. For God's sake, don't give them another hostage." The barrel rose and pointed directly at her.

She bent and retrieved the package, straightened, and stepped towards the house. Luc was halfway to his knees when Samuel grabbed his arm. "Wait, boss.
That was Seb I spotted through the other window."

"Damn it, she's going inside. I've got to—"

Samuel maintained an iron grip on his arm. "Wait, boss. Soon be dark, then we can get close. We'll get them out."

Chapter Eighteen

Eva sidled through the narrow opening allowed by the man behind the gun, and the door slammed shut, catching her skirt. The package was ripped from her hands and someone grabbed her arm and tossed her onto a wooden chair. A strip tore from her skirt and hung in the door. She held her breath, not daring to look and direct the kidnappers' attention towards her pocket. Hand trembling, she slowly moved her fingers down to the torn patch. Cool and solid, the bulge of her gun remained out of sight in her pocket.

She shifted in her seat and eased upright. Shaking fingers brushed hair off her face. In the corner of the flagstone floor below a window, Seb lay trussed with heavy rope. Pale and bruised around the face, he didn't move.

Was that blood on his cheek? In the rapidly dimming light, it was impossible to tell.

"Seb, are you okay?"

A solid body stepped in front and blocked him from her view. Under his right arm he held the dummy package. She tipped her head back and stared into Stefan's bearded face. Cold, dark eyes pinned her to the seat and all the air whooshed from her lungs.

Stefan. Mind blank, she stared at him numbly.

"He not be okay for long if you don't do what you are told." His heavy accent added menace to his threat.

Stefan must have had her under surveillance as soon as she crested that rise on the track. Thank goodness Luc had known where the cottage was. If he'd been in the Jeep when she pulled up, they'd probably have been shot before they got out of the car. Their strategy had bought her enough time to get into the cottage but she prayed Stefan wouldn't open the box immediately.

In her peripheral vision, she saw him raise his left hand.

Lamplight glinted on metal. He had a knife.

Stefan tossed the blade, caught it, hefted it and leaned in close. Cold, sharp metal pressed against the skin of her throat. "Be good if you want your boy safe. Understand, *boss lady*?"

If she nodded, would the knife cut her?

"Do you?" Stefan wanted an answer. She swallowed the lump of fear lodged in her throat and the knife tip stung like a bee. A trickle—of blood?—ran down her neck. She offered a breathless *yes.*

He flicked the knife away and wiped the blade on her skirt. "Good. Now, you stay there. If you good, I not tie you up. If bad, I kill him." He jerked a thumb without looking at Seb's prone body. "Did you tell anyone you were coming here?"

"You told me not to. Please—is Seb okay?"

"For now." Stefan carried the box to the window and stepped over Seb's prone body.

Footsteps rang on the flagstones behind but she didn't dare turn her head.

"Hey, Stefan, this ain't the deal I signed up for. You said no one would get hurt."

Oh, God, it was Kowalski! Sleazebag. No wonder she had taken a dislike to him.

Stefan didn't bother looking at the journalist. He stood to one side of the window and peered into the almost night outside. "Shut up, you fool. I told you, whatever it takes. That necklace is mine." He moved back into the room and stood toe to toe with the reporter, his face thrust into the American's. "What? Did you think I could say I want it and she would hand it over? American fool. I take back what is mine."

"Sure, man, okay. Don't sweat it." Kowalski backed away, palms warding Stefan off. "I just want the story you promised me. It's cool." Stefan returned to look out through the other window.

Dissension in the ranks. How could she use that? Eva risked a quick look around the cottage. Three rooms, kitchen out back, bedroom behind her and the main room where they were grouped. Kowalski had come from the bedroom. Was there anyone in the kitchen?

Directing her attention to Stefan, she asked, "May I have a glass of water, please?"

"What you think this is? Hotel?" Stefan's gruff tone boded badly for Seb and her. He had to be her target if she got the chance. Kowalski didn't seem likely to hurt, let alone kill, anyone.

"I'll get it, Stefan." Kowalski scrambled for the back room and a moment later she heard water gushing from a faucet and the low murmur of voices.

Three of them. Who was the third? Could it be young Ben? He was Seb's friend and the least likely to be a kidnapper. She bided her time and convinced herself they were going to get out of here alive.

Kowalski came back and handed her a glass filled to overflowing with rust-coloured water. It slopped over her skirt as he shoved it at her without a word and retreated into the bedroom. A pistol hung from his right hand as though he had little idea what to do with it. Eva placed the glass under her chair without drinking. At least she now knew there were three men to contend with.

Arrogant but cautious, the Russian surveyed the terrain in front of the cottage. What if he spotted Luc and the boys? Would he kill Seb and her straight away? He slipped the tip of his knife beneath the thick twine of her package and sawed it off. It fell on Seb's chest. Heart in her mouth, she tried to swallow her fear. Seb hadn't moved. She had to be strong for both of them. She had to be strong until Luc rescued them. Because she'd done what he'd told her not to do. Refusal to go into the cottage hadn't been an option. Not at the point of a gun. Now, the best way she could help was to distract Stefan.

"Did you set fire to the shed?"

"Of course." Stefan tossed the answer her way without bothering to look.

"What did you hope to achieve?"

"Frighten you away so I could look for necklace. But you wouldn't go to Martineau's home so I went to airport early on day you took joy flight and nicked oil line on helicopter. Gave me most of evening to search."

At least she knew who was responsible for the *accidents* but knowledge wasn't her main goal. She wanted his attention on her to give Luc the best chance of approaching undetected. Eva edged forward on her chair. "Stefan, why do you think the necklace is yours?"

"Not think, know it is."

"It belonged to my ancestor, Josephine Dubois. How could it be yours?"

Stefan cast her a look filled with loathing and menace and she shrank back in her chair.

"It was given to her by her lover, Ivan. He had no right to give away Russian Imperial jewels to his whore."

Whore? Anger rose at the slur on her ancestor's character. She fisted her hands in her lap and gritted her teeth. How quick men were to label women who dared to love freely, outside of marriage. Like her. Was she carrying Luc's child? Was there another life at risk? She pressed her hands to her stomach and promised her maybe-child protection and love.

"You don't know her husband didn't purchase the necklace for her. He was a wealthy man."

"I know truth. Woman in man's bed destroys his honour. Ivan was a fool and a traitor to Mother Russia." Stefan's attention was firmly on her face as he dug in his pocket and withdrew Josephine's diary. He waved it in her face with a flourish then slapped it on the table by her side.

An oil lamp spilled a small circle of light onto the table while the rest of the room grew dark. Corners filled with threatening shadows that twisted and jumped in macabre dance with each puff of wind over the lamp.

Stefan twitched the curtain into place and crossed to the table. He pulled out a chair, sat and lifted the package, weighing it in his hands. He shook it then placed it in front of him. "Okay, no one's out there. You came alone. Let's check the contents." He ripped off the brown paper wrapping.

Eva shifted on the seat so her body shielded her hand movements. She bunched up the material of her circular skirt into her left hand and felt for the pocket opening with her right. Her fingers closed around the handle of her father's service revolver. An Abbott didn't allow others to do their work.

Stefan fumbled with the string on the inner wrapping, grabbed his knife and slit it open, revealing the locked jewellery box Eva had selected to serve as the dummy case. Since neither of them had seen the real necklace, she hoped Stefan expected something similar to what she'd given him.

"It's locked. Where is key?" His black eyes bored into her, demanding she surrender it. He pushed back his chair and stood. "Well?" His gaze flicked to her chest and the gold necklace that slipped out of sight between her breasts. Did he think the key was on her chain? *Please don't let him frisk me.*

"I...it's... I forgot to bring it." Could he tell she was lying?

Luc had suggested leaving the key on her kitchen table beside the ball of twine. "Anything to slow him down."

His gaze narrowed on her. He drew the knife toward him, picked it up and tapped it in his palm. "You forgot?"

She nodded. "I was anxious about Seb and I left it on the table at home."

"Humph. No matter." He turned back to the box, inserted the tip of the knife under the lid and twisted. The lid sprang open and the lock flew through the air and landed with a metallic thud on the floor between them.

He pulled the oil lamp closer and prodded the satin bag she used to protect her silk stockings. His lips pulled up in what might pass for a smile. "I know you have it all the time. Like you, I would not admit if I had it. Now—I wait too long for this moment."

He pulled open the drawstring of the bag and shoved his big hand inside.

Eva tightened her grip on her revolver. She inhaled and exhaled as Luc had taught her to do, visualising the shot she would make when Stefan discovered the deception.

Seconds slowed into micro-seconds as though she watched a movie flick past, frame by slow frame. Stefan frowned and withdrew his hand from the bag, his big fist clenched around the contents. He dropped the bag and leaned down close to the lamplight.

Eva eased off the chair and backed towards the door, eyes fixed on his profile. His big fist opened. There, in the middle of his palm, lay a single emerald on a gold chain. Her mother's necklace and the only emerald she'd ever owned.

For one frozen moment, Stefan and the necklace formed a tableau she would never forget.

With a roar, he hurled the jewellery into the corner. It whizzed past her head. His fist closed around his knife. "Bitch. I want Imperial necklace. Where is it?"

Kowalski and Ben raced into the room, the boy unarmed. He cast a look across at Seb and went green around the gills.

She swallowed the lump in her throat and nodded at the box. "In the lid, the key."

Stefan glared at her, his eyes never leaving her face as he reached for the box. He raised it to chest height and flicked a glance inside. "What is key for?"

"The necklace—the Imperial necklace—is too valuable to be kept at home. It's in a bank safety deposit box."

"Why you give other one? What purpose?"

"As a sign of good faith. It's Sunday. The bank isn't open on the weekend."

"So, we wait. In morning, you go to bank and bring it here.

If not, young boss dead."

She whipped up the gun, clapped both hands around it and pointed it at Stefan's heart. This close there was no way she would miss. "Stay back, all of you. You should have believed me, Stefan. I told you I don't have it."

"I not believe you. Now, I kill boy. Then you." He lunged towards Seb.

Eva aimed and squeezed the trigger.

Chapter Nineteen

Darkness provided cover as Luc, Samuel, and three of the boys crawled up to the house on the blind side. Luc flattened himself against the wall and peered around. There was one gun in this corner room and at least one more rifle inside. He peered across the house front to the far side. A patch of black, deeper than the night, slipped into place beneath the far window. Samuel was in place. It wouldn't be much longer.

Hugging the wall, Samuel edged closer to the window while he commando-crawled below the window on his side and took up a position between the window and door. Surprise was crucial. Samuel peered around the ledge, ready to make the call when he saw what was going on inside. Faint light lit his face from within the room. Luc tensed, waiting for Samuel's signal.

A gunshot exploded inside. Luc spun around and kicked in the door. It splintered and gave way, banging against the side wall. He charged through, gun at the ready, as Samuel smashed the window glass and trained his gun on a figure that emerged from the back of the house. He yelled, "Drop it!" and a small firearm clattered to the floor.

Eva was standing, smoking gun in hand and a fierce expression on her face. Like a lioness.

In the corner, Seb lay bound and unmoving. Standing between Eva and him, Stefan Lutchenko clutched his left shoulder. Blood oozed between his fingers. His left hand released its grip on a knife. The blade fell, point first and clanged on the flagstones.

Luc trained his gun on the Russian and moved between Eva and the kidnapper.

Seb groaned and tossed his head from side to side. The sound seemed to release Eva from her warrior stance. She raced past Lutchenko without looking at him and dropped to her knees beside the boy. She eased him up and rested his head on her lap and stroked his cheek. "Seb, are you hurt? Speak to me."

Luc kicked Lutchenko's knife towards Eva. "Use that to cut Seb's ropes. And you"—he turned to the Russian. What he wouldn't give for five minutes alone, bare knuckles, man to man with him—"Attempted murder and kidnap—you can look forward to a very long jail sentence. You won't be seeing the outside of a jail until you're a very old man. As for these other two, aiding and abetting will do for starters."

The younger man's face blanched and he cast a frightened look at Seb and Eva. "He promised no one would get hurt. He promised."

Luc stepped out of the doorway to allow his boys access to the tiny cottage. "Tie them up. The police are on their way." As soon as the three kidnappers were bound and hustled into the bedroom under guard, he lowered his weapon and joined Eva.

Seb sat, head resting on Eva's shoulder. A streak of dried blood marked his temple and cheek. Luc hunkered down in front, slowly moving one finger across Seb's field of vision. Eyes unfocused, Seb was losing the struggle to stay awake.

Gently, Eva probed his hair. "I think he's concussed." She removed her hand. Fresh blood covered her fingertips and she drew a sharp breath.

He took Seb's hand and checked his pulse. It was strong but the concussion needed to be monitored. "Let's get him out of here. I'll drive you to the hospital." He hoisted Seb across his shoulders, fireman-fashion and eased him head first through the door.

Samuel strode up the hill, a cigarette between his fingers. "Hey, boss, Miss Abbott. Police nearly here." He nodded towards the track. Headlights flashed through thick vegetation and the roar of engines carried up the hill.

"Samuel, will you talk to them? Seb needs medical

attention. I'm taking him and Eva to the hospital. We'll stop by the police station when he's out of the woods, maybe in the morning."

"Sure thing, boss."

Eva touched Samuel's arm. "Thank you for all your help. It was a real comfort knowing you and Luc and the boys were out here."

"Glad we could help, miss. Didn't think much of that manager of yours. Unfriendly and poking his nose in where he shouldn't have been."

Eva smiled and headed off down the slope. Luc shifted Seb on his shoulders. The boy was heavier than he looked. Nearly a man. And this experience would make him grow up quickly. "Be sure to tell the police about Lutchenko's attempt to kill Seb. I want that bastard in prison for good. He won't threaten Eva or Seb again."

He strode off, following her to his Jeep. She climbed into the back, and he lowered Seb until his head rested in her lap. "Hang on to him. It's a bumpy road even in daylight. I'll make it as smooth as I can." He started the engine. The first of three police vehicles pulled in behind, blocking his exit while the other two parked in a flurry of dust beyond the gate.

Two officers jumped out, guns trained on them. "Step out of the vehicle, sir. And you too, ma'am."

Luc lifted his hands off the wheel and raised them beside his head. "I'm Lucien Martineau. We called you about the kidnapping. We have an injured boy in the back."

Eva hadn't moved although she had the presence of mind to show her hands. "Officer, my nephew needs to see a doctor. He was kidnapped and—"

One of the officers trained a flashlight on Seb's face then flicked it up at Eva. Pale but determined, she shaded Seb's eyes with her hand. "He needs medical attention. They hit him on the head and he's bleeding."

The younger officer turned to the older and they conferred

briefly. "Thank you, Mr Martineau. We'll radio the hospital to expect you."

"Appreciate it, thanks." Luc climbed into the Jeep as the police vehicle rolled out of the way. "Won't be long, Eva."

Her heart thudded as she paced the hospital corridor. Behind the dark green door, Seb lay, pale and unresponsive after surgery. He hadn't opened his eyes since they'd left the cottage. She wondered if he ever would again.

By the time they'd got him to the hospital, his pulse was erratic and he was bleeding from his ear. Doctors and nurses surrounded him and she was forced to wait outside the emergency ward with only her dark thoughts for company, while Luc disappeared in search of a phone. She wrapped an arm around her waist. Why was it taking so long? Why wouldn't they tell her anything?

Luc appeared in front of her and thrust a cup of coffee into her hand. "Drink. It will be a while before we know how well the operation went." He put an arm around her shoulders and guided her to a chair in the tiny waiting area. She shivered, craving his warmth but not trusting it. Seb had lost a lot of blood. Despite Luc's optimism, she feared the worst.

"Don't beat yourself up all the time. You couldn't have known Lutchenko is a criminal."

Her jaw dropped. She frowned at Luc and snapped her mouth shut. "How did you know what I was thinking?"

"You have a very expressive face. You try to hide behind a mask but you have little tells. You'd be no good at high-stakes poker."

She frowned and shook her head, "Poker? What are you talking about?"

"Look, I hope you won't think I'm speaking out of turn but when the doctor told you how much Seb's operation would cost— well, I'm guessing you don't have that kind of money lying around."

Heat invaded her cheeks and shame. Unless she got that Tourism Board contract, she was going to have to sell the plantation to fund the delicate brain operation. If the hospital would agree to a repayment plan.

And if Seb didn't recover? Her stomach clenched and fatigue gnawed at her brain.

"Can we not talk about this right now?"

"If not now then when? Seb's had the operation and you have to pay for it. Soon. I can help." Luc lifted her coffee cup out of her hands and placed it beside his on the floor beneath his seat. He took both her hands in a loose hold and ran his thumb across her knuckles.

Tired and worried as she was, a thrill ran through her body at his touch. Would it always be this way when he touched her?

"Eva, I know this is a terrible time to ask but under the circumstances—marry me now. We'll get a special license and get married right away. I can help sort everything out and ensure Seb gets the best care. The plantation need not be a worry for you. I'll keep it running."

He'll keep it running if I marry him?

Luc wanted her to give up control of *her* plantation. But Abbotts were self sufficient, independent, and she'd tried so hard to live up to her family responsibilities. His offer was generous but—

Did he love her, even a little?

Her tired brain grappled with the idea of a loveless marriage. *Not completely loveless. I love him.*

Was great sex enough of a foundation to build on? Was she greedy to want it all?

She drew a deep breath. Without his love, she couldn't do it.

She eased her hands out of his hold and looked him in the eyes. "Thank you for your offer, Luc. It's…neighbourly, and I was tempted to accept your proposal, but I can't. Not even on the chance I'm pregnant. It wouldn't be right."

His lips thinned into a grim line. "Is the thought of marrying me so repugnant? I know I'm not your aristocratic gentleman but together we could make a good life here." He stood abruptly and strode to the window.

Her heart longed to go to him, wrap her arms around him, love him.

Tension radiated from every line of his body silhouetted against the bright light. So strong and so alone. Surely she had enough love in her heart for both of them. Couldn't that be enough?

But he didn't love her.

She closed her eyes and tried to breathe through the pain of letting him go. Without love, it could never be. "Luc, you're a good man. But we're wrong together. And I have to look after Seb like his parents would have if they'd lived."

"Do you think I'd stop you doing what you wanted? Is that it, Eva? You don't trust me." His flat tones shredded her already breaking will.

The band around her heart tightened another notch. She had to set him free from the responsibility he had shouldered. "You've been nothing but kind to us since we met."

"Kind?" He spun around and glared, his eyes fierce and dark and filled with pain beneath his frown. "What's between us has nothing to do with *kindness*."

"I admit I'm…very attracted to you. But lust isn't a foundation for a marriage."

"You mean I'm great for a fling but not to settle down with." He shoved his hands in his pockets and looked at the floor. "No, you're right. Lust broke up my parents' marriage. Why would I choose a woman just because I'm in lust with her?" Bitter tones, delivered by the man who had saved her and Seb.

How could she do this to him? He didn't love her so why

did she feel no better than Genevieve, who'd broken his heart. Maybe that was why he couldn't love her. Because he was still in love with the woman who had broken his heart. But she loved him and she could do this for him. She and Seb would start afresh, maybe in Australia.

"You asked me to give you first option if I decided to sell the plantation. I'm selling. Do you want to exercise that option now?"

###

You're a great fuck, Luc. Eva may have phrased it more elegantly but her refusal echoed Genevieve's. And he'd never felt so right with anyone as with her.

How could he have thought she would be different from the others? He'd let down his guard and offered her all that he was but it wasn't enough. *He* wasn't enough. When would he get it into his thick head? His mother's adultery tainted his blood and no woman wanted the risk of marrying into such a family.

Ironic really, that his complaint to his father had been how he didn't trust women when all the time it was *him* they didn't trust. But his compensation was that Eva had offered him the Benson place.

Definitely ironic.

Land was cold comfort when the woman he loved couldn't get beyond what had brought them together in the first place. And that now divided them.

Bittersweet and ironic.

Chapter Twenty

Eva feathered her fingers over Seb's cheek as he lay in the hospital bed. A lighter bandage now replaced the heavy post-operative one, but his face was thinner and paler. Combined with his stubble and the frown between his brows, he looked older, highlighting the similarity to his father. If he'd been awake he wouldn't have let her touch him like that, but he was still in the induced coma dictated by the doctor to allow his head trauma time to heal.

"Oh, Seb, please be well. We have such a lot to talk about and decisions to make, and I really want you to be part of it this time."

Except the decision to sell Benson's place. Her hand clenched in her skirt. There'd been no choice in that if medical expenses were to be met but the sense of betrayal left a sour taste in her mouth.

"I hope you don't hold it against me but I couldn't marry Luc, even to save your inheritance, my love. I can't bear the thought of being with him knowing he doesn't love me."

The door to the room opened. Surreptitiously, she swiped her cheeks and hunted for her handkerchief.

Seb's surgeon stood there, his usually stern expression relieved by a smile. "Ah, Miss Abbott. I was hoping to catch you today. Would you join me for a few minutes?"

"Certainly, doctor." She cast a glance at Seb and patted his hand as she stood. "I'll be back soon."

She slipped through the door and the doctor closed it behind her. Slightly embarrassed at being caught talking to an unconscious audience, she asked, "I'm sure he can hear me, doctor.

I keep talking to him and telling him what's happening. Do you think it helps?"

"I'm certain it does no harm and it may be that he hears you on a subconscious level. Keep talking to him." Dr Andrews led her to the end of the corridor and opened the door into his office. "Please take a seat, Miss Abbott. There are a few things to discuss."

First and foremost would be payment of the bills. She wondered why the hospital hadn't asked for payment before now but was thankful that they hadn't. "I've arranged for the sale of our property. The proceeds should be available soon, and I'll be able to pay the bills for Seb's operation and accommodation."

"Please, don't worry yourself. Your solicitor has already deposited sufficient funds." Dr Andrews shook his head and opened a yellow envelope. He took out Seb's patient notes and flicked through them. "Besides, that isn't what I want to talk about. I hope you haven't been worried about that?" He smiled, removed his glasses, and polished them on his handkerchief.

"A little. That was good of him. He didn't mention it to me."

"Perhaps he felt you had enough to cope with already. Now, in layman's terms, we've taken Seb off the medication that kept him in the coma state."

Surprise, relief, elation surged through her, along with a rush of gratitude for the doctor. "You mean he'll wake up soon?"

"I do, and don't be surprised if he answers questions you've asked while he's been under." Dr Andrews's smile hadn't left his face.

She wanted to bounce out of her seat and do a war dance in celebration. They'd have to have a party at home, invite friends and—neighbours.

Bittersweet, the irony of what they'd traded for Seb's recovery hit her. Except they wouldn't have a home to go to. She should have asked Luc if they could rent the house until Seb had recovered.

Dr Andrews continued. "We believe he will be fine to go home with you within a week. Will that suit you?"

Laugh, cry, or both, Eva didn't know what to do with the news. She blinked back tears. "Thank you, doctor. That's the best news I could have asked for."

"He will, of course, need to convalesce for a time. Rest, no excitement. I believe you have been staying in the hostel nearby while Seb has been with us?"

"That's right. I couldn't bear to be away from him."

"Will you go home to prepare for his return?"

"No. I'll wait until we can go home together." She trusted Luc would give them a few weeks.

Luc shovelled the last of the mulch into place and stepped out of the garden bed. He straightened and wiped his forearm across his forehead. "Samuel, tell the boys to be sure to tidy up and get those lights strung before they pack up."

"Sure, boss. They're looking forward to having Seb home again. *And* Miss Abbott."

Luc grunted and turned away, but not before he saw a huge grin spread across Samuel's face. What did he expect? A bloody miracle? And wasn't that what he was hoping for? His recent visit and discussion with Seb had revived hope that not all was lost. In fact, Seb had offered interesting observations for a patient who had been kept in an induced coma.

"I'm heading home to clean up and get changed. I'll bring Annie back with the food by four o'clock."

"We'll have everything ready. Gonna be a nice surprise for Seb. *And* Miss Abbott."

"Wipe that goddamn grin off your face and stop saying *Miss Abbott* like that."

"Okay, boss."

Luc climbed into his Jeep and started the engine. He looked

over the garden he and the boys had rushed to complete before Eva and Seb returned home this afternoon. In a few months the plants would have gained height and the perfumes would scent the night air. Like they did in her old home, he hoped. Would she understand what it meant? What he wanted to say but couldn't find words for?

Eva drove up the driveway, a mixture of hope and sadness churning in her stomach. Hope that Seb would make a full recovery, and despair that she hadn't kept his inheritance intact for him. If only she had looked after him better. Seb had nearly died because of the choices she'd made.

"Look, Evie!" As they rounded the last bend, he pointed at the line up of vehicles parked along the upper stretch of driveway. "We've got visitors."

Eva sniffed back her self-pity. It would not be allowed to affect his homecoming. "Looks like some of your friends heard you're coming home today. Oh, dear, there won't be anything to eat or drink in the house."

Carefully, she drove between cars to the shed and parked. Seb climbed out unaided and came around to offer her his arm. "Leave the bags for now, Evie. Let's go see who's here."

They rounded the corner and walked slowly up to the house. If he leaned a little heavily on her arm, she was just happy that he was alive and walking and talking. But something had shifted within him. He was a man. He had much still to learn but suddenly she knew he would be fine.

Long tables set up under the trees groaned with food, the tablecloth anchored by a large punch bowl at each end. Coloured lights hung between the veranda posts and through the branches of the nearby trees. And gathered around the tables were Seb's friends, come to welcome him home.

Home. Not for much longer. Far better to have told him earlier, before—

Panic set in as she spotted Luc standing at the far end of the table. Tall, dark, and unutterably gorgeous, Luc stood beside a grinning Samuel. Even across yards of grass and over the heads of young men, she was aware of his intense gaze on her. Her cheeks warmed as he watched their progress. He made no move towards them but raised his glass and drank.

Seb's friends surrounded him, and she released her hold on his arm. Moe led him to a chair then dropped onto another seat while the others sprawled into casual positions on the grass around him.

Before Luc had a chance to say anything about the sale to Seb, she was going to ask if they could rent the house for a few weeks. Skirting the group of young men, she headed toward Luc. She had him in her sights when a blue and green Hawaiian shirt stepped into her path and Jack held out his hand.

Jack Lyons must have a wardrobe of many-coloured Hawaiian shirts. She shook his hand and managed a smile for the real estate agent. "Hello, Jack. Long time no see."

"True. Hey, I found you a manager by the way. He can come over tomorrow if you want to interview him."

"After the last one you found for me, I don't think I'd trust your choice again. But I won't be needing another manager."

"What do you mean after the last one? I haven't sent anyone else."

Shock whacked her like a duping wave. "What about Stefan Lutchenko? He led me to understand you'd sent him."

"Never heard of the man until Luc told me about Seb's kidnapping."

So, there was yet one more thing she'd gotten wrong.

Jack touched her arm, preventing her getaway. "Anyway, I hear congratulations are in order." He presented her with a glass of punch then picked up a cup for himself and toasted her with it. "Well done."

"I beg your pardon? For what?" Getting her nephew

kidnapped and nearly killed?

"The contract. You and Luc jointly won the Tourism contract."

"Oh, my." A contract and no property. Could the universe dump any more irony on her head?

"Surely you've been told by now? What did Luc say about that? Or doesn't it matter, now you two are—"

"Are what? There's nothing going on between Luc and me."

"Oh, come on, Eva. Everyone could see you two were going to make a match of it at the Planters' Ball. Hey, you wouldn't even let me kiss you goodnight when I drove you home and let me tell you, that doesn't happen to me—ever!"

His optimistic outlook on life would have brought a smile to her face if her heart weren't broken. Over Jack's shoulder, she caught sight of Luc. "Whatever you think you know, you're wrong. End of story."

"Fine, keep me out in the cold. But I know Luc. He won't give up on the woman he loves." Jack grinned wryly. "I never really had a chance, did I?"

Did everyone expect Luc and her to be getting married? Did they all think he was in love with her? If only he were. She pasted on a social smile. "Excuse me, Jack. I've got to…"

Got to get out of here. Forget Luc, find a place to sit, breathe, think. Luc didn't love her and no amount of wishing would make it so. Jack didn't know what he was talking about.

She headed for the veranda on the far side of the house and splendid isolation. Laughter and the shouts of young men in party mode followed her into the shadows as she climbed the side steps. She leaned on the railing, her head resting against her palm, and stared into the garden.

She blinked and examined the ground below.

A garden? Since when had there been a garden here?

Gardenias, roses, and small plants that looked suspiciously

like foxgloves nestled in well-mulched soil. With careful attention, they would be a splendid display in a few months. Not a rival to the gardens at Bellerose, but a gorgeous reminder of another place and time. Except she wouldn't be here to enjoy it.

"Do you like it, Eva?" Luc's approach had been lost in her floral reverie. He stood close, but made no move to touch her.

Bereft, she curled her fingers around the railing and stared into the dark garden. "It will be beautiful and the perfumes of these flowers will be glorious. But why create a garden here rather than at your place? What if your new tenants don't look after it?"

"There won't be any tenants. The owner will be living here and, I have it on good authority, loves English gardens."

"I don't understand. You're the owner, aren't you?" A horrible thought occurred to her. When Luc had originally offered for the Benson property, it had been for the land only. "Have you sold the house separately? Oh, dear. I meant to ask you if Seb and I could stay on, as paying tenants of course, until he's recuperated."

"It's not available for rent."

A chill settled in her bones as the bottom fell out of her world. They didn't have anywhere to live, Seb would have to move away from his good friends, and she'd probably have to sell off what remained of their past at Bellerose.

How could she have made such a mess of their lives?

She wrapped her arms around her stomach and struggled to breathe through the constriction around her chest. She forced air into her lungs and pushed out the question she should have already settled with Luc. "How long do we have before the new owner wants to move in?"

"The owner is here now."

"What? Then why the welcome home party if we have no home? Do we have to leave immediately?" Heart hammering, she fought the dizzy sensation that threatened to spill the little she'd managed to eat at lunch.

Luc took out a folded paper from his pocket and handed it

to her. She accepted it gingerly, as though it would bite.

"Maybe this will explain it." He leaned against the railing and crossed his arms.

She unfolded the paper. In the dim light falling through the window behind she scanned the first page. "It's a title deed."

"To this property."

"In the name of—Evangeline Catherine Abbott, the property known as...*Bellerose Plantation*?" A sense of unreality descended, fuelled by the night and stress and yearning for the impossible. Could it really be her home now and forever more?

She met Luc's gaze. "Really?"

"The estate is yours."

"I don't understand. Dr Andrews said my solicitor had arranged payment of the hospital bills from the sale to you."

He grimaced. "A little white lie and, I promise, the last one I'll ever tell you. The sale as such never went through. Jack's missed out on a commission but I doubt he'll mind this time."

"*You* paid Seb's bills? And you've given up...*Bellerose*...to me? But why?"

He unfolded his arms and took a step toward her but pulled himself up short. He dropped his arms stiffly by his side and looked intently into her eyes. "How else can I show you, make you believe, it's you I want to marry. I don't want this place. Just you. I made the garden to show you—to tell you. I love you, Eva. And if you're of a mind to form a partnership with me, we can do great things for tourism with these two plantations. After all, *we* jointly won the Tourism Board contract."

Full of wonder at her blindness, she looked into Luc's dark eyes and saw her love reflected in his. "I didn't think you loved me. How could I not have seen? This garden is made with love. Your love. Oh, Luc, I love you, too."

She flung herself into his arms and sought his mouth. Locked in his embrace, she hardly heard the music and party, or saw the night falling.

Spots of gaily swinging colour glowed into life in the trees. A moment later, the lights on the veranda turned on, glowing like a wonderland.

Luc kissed a path from her lips to her ear and nuzzled her ear lobe. "Is that a *yes* then?"

"Yes, please. I want to marry you, Luc. As soon as possible."

"Will next week be soon enough? I think Annie needs a little time to prepare our wedding cake or she'll never forgive me."

Eva blinked back happy tears. "I don't know yet if I'm pregnant or not but I want to have your children. I want to make a real family together."

Luc grinned and pulled her closer. "*That* we can start on tonight."

Epilogue

1961

Caroline Martineau gurgled and waved her little fists against her father's mouth. He dropped kisses on each hand then lay back on the bed and blew a raspberry against her stomach. She gave him a gummy smile and grabbed his nose.

Eva entered the bedroom carrying a frothy confection of christening gown trimmed with pink ribbons in her hands. "Time to get dressed, sweetheart. If Daddy will hold you still so I can just slip this over your head—" She kneeled on the bed beside him and positioned the opening of the gown above their five-month-old daughter's head.

He sat Caroline on his chest and watched as his wife slid the garment over their little girl's body. As she fastened the gown, her head was level with Caroline's. Twin pairs of green eyes met his. Caroline bounced on his chest, grabbed a handful of gown, and shoved it in her mouth.

Carefully balancing the baby in one arm, he snaked the other around Eva's waist and pulled her against his body. Her breasts, full and heavy since birthing their daughter, pressed into his chest. The smell of milk combined with Eva's scent aroused him. Hell, everything about her aroused him. Predictably, his body came to attention as it always did when Eva was near. He nuzzled her ear. "Happy first anniversary, darling."

"Happy anniversary." Snuggled against his shoulder, she tipped her head up and kissed him lingeringly.

"Do you think anyone would notice if we were late to Caroline's christening?" His question was muffled by Eva's mouth.

"What did you have in mind?" She nibbled on his lower lip and ran her stockinged foot up his calf. Her knee pressed against his erection in a slow, erotic slide that rated high on the pain-pleasure borderline.

He groaned and slid his hand down to caress her thigh through her skirt. "Eva, you're killing me here. Let me put Caro in her cot so I can wish you a proper happy anniversary."

"Unless you can set a new speed record, we'll have to wait. Henri and Jayne were coming up the driveway as I came in."

"Give them Caroline to play with. She'll entertain them." His hand stroked along the curve from her bottom and pulled her blouse out of her skirt. He touched bare skin before she sighed and sat up.

"They've got Seb with them and Jack is already on the front veranda nursing a celebratory whiskey. He blames me for his lack of a drinking partner. Go and say hello while I tidy my hair."

He grabbed her wrist and sat up beside her while Caroline exchanged chewing her pink ribbons for one of his shirt buttons. "Ahem, give me a few minutes; I'm not in a fit state to greet our guests at the moment."

"And I am? Smudged lipstick and bedroom hair aren't exactly *de rigueur* for a christening. Or greeting one's in-laws." She tucked in her top and smoothed her hands down her skirt, twitching it back into place. Reflected in the mirror, her smile blazed out at him as she unwound her hair and grabbed her hairbrush. "Give me one minute and I'll take Caro out to say hello to her family."

"Are you going to wear your hair up? I like it when you do. I can nibble on your neck."

"You like it up so you can play as you lose all my hairpins." She shoved another pin in and turned her head to either side, checking her hastily re-pinned hairstyle.

God, he loved her hair. Up or down, it was all the same to

him. What mattered most was that Eva had gained the confidence to choose because she was secure and happy in his love. He kissed his daughter's soft auburn curls then shifted her to his other arm. Jiggling her gently, he patted her back as he watched Eva touch up her lipstick. What had he done to get so lucky?

"Are you going to give Seb the diary tonight?"

She stopped in the middle of painting her lips and met his gaze. "I think he'll be happy to continue the quest for the emerald necklace. He's still got dreams of finding it one day."

"Are you sure you don't want to go to New Orleans to continue the search? We could combine it with a holiday if you wanted to." He eased a ribbon out of the baby's mouth and smoothed her gown into place.

Eva met his gaze and tipped her head to the side as she studied him. "Do you want to look for it?"

"I've got my treasure right here. You and Caro are all I've ever wanted. I just didn't know it for a while. But if you want to look for Josephine's necklace—"

She came to him then and kneeled between his legs. His arousal, which had begun to ease, gained a resurgence of interest and urgency.

"Luc, the possible existence of Josephine's necklace was enough to almost lose my nephew. I'm not superstitious but I don't want it and I don't want Caroline to have to worry about it. Seb can look after the diary. If he decides to pursue the necklace, that's his decision. Besides"—she kissed one corner of his mouth—"where would I wear a fabulously rich and gorgeous piece of jewellery like that?" She kissed the other side of his mouth and sat her delectable bottom in his lap.

He raised an eyebrow and grinned. "You could always wear it to bed. According to Marilyn Monroe, one should always have something on."

Eva chuckled. "She was talking about the radio."

"Are you sure you don't want Caro to go and entertain the

family?"

"It would look a little obvious. But I tell you what, hold that thought for now and tonight, I'll wear my emerald pendant to bed, just for you."

"Nothing but the necklace?"

She peeked sideways at him and a seductive smile hovered around her lips. "Well, I might put the radio on as well."

"Have I told you how much I love you?"

She nodded and went into his arms making a close threesome with their daughter. "Every day since we married."

"And I'm going to tell you every day of our lives. I love you, Eva Martineau, and tonight, I'm going to show you just how much."

"Promise?"

"Promise."

The End

Want to know when Susanne Bellamy's next books will be released?
Follow her on:

Bookbub: https://www.bookbub.com/authors/susanne-bellamy
OR
On Facebook:
https://www.facebook.com/susannebellamyauthor/

Read on for a sneak peek of **High Stakes**

Prologue

Sydney, Australia

John Chan faced his father across the antique rosewood desk. Eyes black and lustreless as coal pinned him to the parquet floor. Sleek, satin lapels contrasted with his snow-white tuxedo, and the benign smile he'd bestowed on guests gathered to celebrate his birthday in the marquee below was wiped from his face. Loss of face, especially for the eldest son of the head of family, was unacceptable. He bowed his head and waited for his father to pronounce sentence.

"You allowed her into your office because you let desire for this woman overrule your head. The woman accessed your computer. She escaped. We may be compromised."

"Father, I regret—"

"For a woman." Disgust leached through his words, pitching his voice higher than normal.

It didn't matter that John had increased profits since taking over operations in Sydney. Endangering the family and the business meant his life was forfeit. If his father so wished.

"Third Uncle wants your balls stuffed in your mouth. Second Uncle prefers a visit to the shark tank."

Of course. A bullet to his temple would be considered weakness.

Bile rose in John's throat. Hands gripped tightly together, he tried to swallow the lump of fear threatening to block his response. Now was not the time to show emotion. Now was the time for quick thinking, and for negotiation. What could he offer in exchange for his life?

"I have a contact in the Bureau. May I protect my family by accessing my resources?"

His father shifted on his seat. Red and gold brocade rustled, and shimmered in the low light preferred by his ageing eyes. He tapped one gnarled index finger on the wooden arm of the chair. When it stopped, John raised his eyes to meet his father's.

"Do this, and perhaps your uncles and I will let you live." His father dismissed him with a single flick of his hand. As though he was no more than a fly.

The woman he had sought to win as his mistress had brought him to this.

Anger seared his gut as John bowed and backed out of his father's office. Luxury and all the clothes wealth could afford had been offered but the woman had played him for a fool. Humiliation would be heaped on her tenfold. She would pay dearly.

He pulled his phone from his pocket and unlocked it with his thumbprint. Scrolling through his contacts, the tremor in his fingers filled him with shame. When the code name appeared, he stabbed the screen and waited. Hand in pocket, he peered through the window. Rivulets of rain blurred his view of the formal garden, and red Poinciana leaves bled into a green bush.

The connection rang four times, as it always did. "What do you want now? I told you, she went to the airport where our tail lost her."

His contact had never shown him respect. One day, when his usefulness was over, John would take pleasure in putting a bullet into Iceman's brain.

But not yet.

"You have one chance. Find her. Kill her."

Chapter One

Jake Harris crossed his scuffed trekking boots and touched his whisky glass to the UN commissioner's. Damn if the man didn't keep the best supply this side of Everest. He sipped, welcoming the burn of island peat on his tongue, down his throat, in his gut. Not one drop had touched his lips in two months. Not since he'd found his brother in the garage.

Hanging like a frozen side of beef.

Dead.

The memory slammed through him with the force of an avalanche, and the whisky soured in the black pit of his soul.

Peter. Baby brother. Coke-head.

Dead.

He set the crystal tumbler on the mahogany desk with a thunk. Lamplight lit the lower half of his body and he leaned back, praying his face was in deep shadow. If—when—he got his hands on those responsible for Pete's death, he'd bring them down. By any means. "What do you need from me, Mr Nicholls?"

Grey jacket sleeves rode up and revealed pristine white cuffs. The commissioner folded soft hands on the desk, and his socially-polite, upwardly-mobile smile, the smile of the career diplomat, was packed away. "I understand you're a man of few words. I suppose that's why you chose field work over the diplomatic corps."

The commissioner's plummy tones grated. Jake preferred lilting Nepalese voices to Oxford city-slickness. "I'm leaving Kathmandu in the morning."

"Impatient, Mr Harris?"

"I have new field agents to train." In truth, his second-in-charge in the south-east Asia division of the Bureau was responsible for inductions, but Jake needed space. Room to breathe, open air, and pushing himself to the limit so he could snatch a few hours of dreamless sleep. So far the plan had failed more than it had succeeded.

"Fine, let's cut to the chase. Doctor Westcott is heading up the trail towards Everest Base Camp. Ostensibly on holiday." Nicholls drew a folder towards him.

"And?"

"It's the second part of her trip we hold concerns about."

"Congratulations on solving all the major world problems." He didn't bother trying to subdue his sarcastic side. Sarcasm was good. Sarcasm masked his I'm-going-through-hell face and made taking his next breath, and the next, and the next, possible.

Bitter sarcasm was all he had left.

Because he'd failed. Failed to protect one of the few people he cared about.

Nicholls' hooded eyes fixed on Jake and the sharp plane of his nose lowered as if he were a bird dropping from the sky on hapless prey. Jake glared right back at the commissioner and to hell with protocol. He didn't give a damn if he pissed the man off. He didn't give a damn about anything.

Nicholls fiddled with the knot of his tie. "Doctor Westcott has applied for a research permit to visit the Dolpa region." Jake flicked through memories of his only trip to the central province. "It's remote, difficult to access, and entry permits are expensive and restricted. Not many trekkers go there. What's the concern?"

"Her specialty. Biological chemistry."

"So? I don't see the connection."

Nicholls leaned back and a smug smile tugged at the corners of his mouth. "Need to know basis, Harris."

Jake thought about telling Nicholls to take his intrigue and shove it where the sun didn't shine. The words teetered on the springboard of his tongue, raw, harsh, bitter. He couldn't give a flying fuck. Not when he had a mountain of paperwork, and a group of raw recruits to whip into shape. "I'm head of drug enforcement operations for the region. Who the hell do you think needs to know if not me?"

Nicholls pursed his lips and tapped his fingers on the closed folder. "This case requires top security clearance."

"Which I have. So—she's a biological chemist. What's the connection?"

"Her work involves research and synthesising compounds."

"Making what? Who for, and why here?"

"That's the problem; we don't know."

"Is Doctor Westcott flying in or trekking?"

Nicholls' internal struggle—to stand firm or answer—drew twin lines of battle between his eyebrows. "What difference does it make?"

A flicker of pleasure licked through Jake. Poncy desk jockey didn't know everything. "Have you ever trekked, Mr Nicholls?"

"Not really my cup of tea." Nicholls' clipped tone dismissed the absurd notion. He picked up a pen and patterned the print label on the folder in a series of jabs. The pen stopped, point down amid a mess of blue dots.

"Why is her mode of travel important?" The question was dragged from him like a dentist pulling a bad tooth.

Jake reached for his glass and took a leisurely mouthful. Nicholls' ignorance of transport within Nepal betrayed his inexperience, but it gave Jake the edge to prise out more details about the woman.

"How she travels determines how much and what can be carried. Unless I know more about what I'm meant to be looking for, I can't help you." He tossed back the last mouthful of whisky. "That's a smooth drop. Don't mind if I have another." Warmth spread through his belly and he poured two fingers' into his glass and sat back.

An antique clock chimed the quarter hour and the echoes hung heavily as Nicholls appeared to deliberate. Finally, he spoke. "Drugs."

The single word blazed like a neon light in the night. Jake's breath caught on the sharp rock of grief lodged in his throat, his stomach clenched. His hands fisted on his knees, and a bongo-beat accelerated in his brain: *Revenge—Peter—revenge—Peter— revenge.*

"You were instrumental in breaking up an international supply line out of Afghanistan last month. I believe the leader, Al-Kohari was killed?"

"Yes." The word shot out like the bullet that put the drug lord beyond reach of justice. The legal kind, at least. Jake's only regret was Al-Kohari had been the key to finding and proving the Australian connection. Without him . . .

Nicholls leaned back. "Nepal isn't exactly drug territory but if Doctor Westcott is involved, we need to know."

"If she's involved, I'll bring her in."

Nicholls capped the pen. "The doctor dined with John Chan in Sydney a few days before she arrived in Kathmandu. Chan is the eldest son of a family with Asian drug links. He met the doctor at an upmarket restaurant on Sydney's Circular Quay."

Jake's heart stuttered then began a mad thumping. The Chan cartel was likely Peter's supplier. He could still see his younger brother's face, purple and obscene above the noose. Jake forced his lungs to breathe. His hand clenched the glass and he downed the whisky in a single mouthful.

"This was taken by an undercover agent tailing Chan." Nicholls opened the folder and handed over an enlarged photo.

Beneath heavy, long, black curls, the woman's delicate expression appeared intent on her dinner companion. She was beautiful. His dispassionate gaze began cataloguing details; from the tilt of her head to the thigh-high slit in her black dress, sex appeal oozed from the woman.

"You said she was dining with Chan. Do you think it was business or pleasure?" Jake tipped the photo towards the desk lamp. "Have you got a magnifier?"

Nicholls took an old-fashioned magnifying glass from his drawer and handed it across the desk. "By the look of her I'd say pleasure, but this was the only time the operative saw them alone together."

Jake examined the photograph closely, paying attention to a mark on the woman's thigh, visible in the thigh-split of the slim-fitting black dress.

A tattoo. Maybe a snake or a gecko. He studied her features, memorising them. Any link to the Chans ensured he would take on this assignment. "So how does her trip to Dolpa fit in with this Sydney drug cartel?"

"We suspect a connection. Her visa states the trip is for research. Loopholes in the laws of both our countries allow the legal importation of certain *natural* drugs, which are then recombined. Some of the ingredients in recombined form are responsible for the recent spate of deaths in your capital cities. And mine."

Jake set the photo and magnifier on the desk. "The Chans are at the centre of it?"

"In Sydney, almost certainly."

"Paul Rimmer and I worked undercover in Sydney before I was promoted to head up the Asian bureau. At last contact, he hinted he was onto someone involved in the local trade."

And now Nicholls was handing him a connection to that underworld family. If it was the last thing he did he would find this woman who had allied herself with the Chinese drug cartel and he would extract the truth. And if she was involved in manufacturing and research . . . Jake's hand fisted on his knee.

"Too many young lives are being cut short." Nicholls' comment lacked real emotion. But bureaucratic say-the-right-thing blah hit Jake hard.

Peter would never grow up, grow old, grow anything. He had ceased to exist except in Jake's memory, and as a black and white statistic on a government department's page.

Grief sank in Paul's gut like a boulder, free-falling down—down—down—into a bottomless chasm.

But he couldn't afford the luxury of time to grieve. Time in which the drug family would set up a new supplier, find new supply lines, shatter more families. He pulled himself together, locked his grief down tighter than an airport on terrorist alert. Peter's death would not go unavenged.

"So this doctor is working for the cartel?"

"That, Harris, is what we want you to find out. Observation only for the time being, but we want to know what the Dolpa connection is. If you confirm a link to the Chans, bring her in." Nicholls closed the folder and shoved it across the desk. "We want eyes on her as soon as possible, before she makes contact with anyone. How quickly can you reach Everest Base Camp?"

"I'll fly in by helicopter tomorrow and backtrack until I find her. Before she reaches Everest, I'll catch her."

And if the doctor was working for the drug family, he would make her pay.

Other Books

Visit Susanne's website to see more books:

http://www.susannebellamy.com/books-by-susanne-bellamy.html

About the Author

I love travel—new places, new faces, different cultures and endless possibilities. I've cruised from Australia to Britain and back through the Suez Canal when I was a child, trekked in Nepal and Vietnam, lived briefly in Noumea, visited western Europe and west coast America among other places. Let me repeat—I love travel! And history.

People's stories fascinate me. Past and present lives and relationships and the mysterious ways Fate works. Even how I met my husband—Fate. Wonderful and mysterious.

And so my stories explore the wonderful and mysterious ways in which people meet. I should probably thank the flat-mate who locked me out of my new house years ago, which led directly to meeting my husband. But that's another story!
I am a member of the Romance Writers of Australia and love to hear from fellow romance authors and readers alike.

Read more at: http://www.susannebellamy.com/